I0610440

# Shadow Dancer

Tangled Souls Book One

Macie Cage

This book is a work of fiction. Names, characters, places, and incidents are either the product of the author's imagination or are used fictitiously. Any resemblance to actual persons, living or dead, events, or locales is entirely coincidental.

Shadow Dancer
Copyright © 2019, Macie Cage.

All Rights Reserved.

Cover design by germancreative on fiverr.com
Edited by Ashley Elliott

Paperback (ISBN-13): 978-1-7336539-2-3

Second Edition

# Shadow Dancer

# Table of Contents

Chapter One .......................................................................1

Chapter Two .................................................................35

Chapter Three ...............................................................58

Chapter Four .................................................................69

Chapter Five..................................................................81

Chapter Six ...................................................................99

Chapter Seven...............................................................115

Chapter Eight................................................................139

Chapter Nine.................................................................152

Chapter Ten ..................................................................160

Chapter Eleven..............................................................171

Chapter Twelve..............................................................179

Chapter Thirteen ...........................................................191

Chapter Fourteen ..........................................................210

Chapter Fifteen .............................................................218

Epilogue.......................................................................227

*Blood is thicker than water.*

# Chapter One
Month of the Rat 26, 407 HE

"Caiden, I have a surprise for you."

The young prince turned towards the newcomer, instantly brightening, and scrambling to his feet to greet his father. The man grinned, ruffling the mess of red curls as the boy hugged him around the waist.

"Is it a present?" the boy asked, blue eyes wide and sparkling with excitement.

His father chuckled. "I suppose you could say that. It is your sixth birthday after all." He gestured to someone out of view, and Caiden leaned around the man's legs to see his father's best friend and personal servant standing outside the door.

Ansom smiled, strands of black hair falling over his whiskey colored eyes before they were quickly corrected. "Good evening, Your Highness. I hope we aren't interrupting."

"Um, good evening." Caiden tried to enunciate his words with the same refined articulation but failed.

A shuffle of movement drew the child's attention to another boy who stood behind his father's advisor. They examined each other for a long moment.

"Caiden, this is Evander. He will be your servant from this day forward, just like Ansom is for me."

Ansom stepped aside as Caiden wandered closer, leaving the now fidgeting child completely exposed. Evander glanced around in a panic before straightening up and waiting while Caiden circled him.

"Hey, do you know how to play Knights and Dragons?" the prince asked curiously, peering up at the older boy.

"Um, no?" Evander responded hesitantly.

Caiden grinned and grabbed his hand. "That's okay! It's real easy. I'll teach you!"

The king chuckled as his son dragged his new servant over to the toys. He turned to leave, beckoning for Ansom to follow him into the hall. The pair would do nicely.

--†--

## Fourteen Years Later
### Month of the Griffin 10, 421 HE

"Evander." The man in question looked up at the Royal Tutor as he trudged across the courtyard. "Where is Prince Caiden?" Luten was sweating in his robes, greying hair falling out of its tie and into his reddening face.

"I don't know." *Badgering old fool.* Evander shifted, making his seat on the ground a bit more comfortable in preparation for the ear blistering lecture.

"Lying now, are we?" The tutor glared, leaning down so his face was mere inches from the servant's. "Tell me where he is. If you don't, you'll be cleaning my study for the next week in addition to your usual—" his eyes narrowed, "why would a lowly servant possess jewelry such as that?"

Evander raised a hand to the tiny golden hoop that dangled from his earlobe. *Damn it all.* "Prince Caiden—"

"Of course," the tutor sneered, "that is something he would do. Give it here."

Evander felt his expression start to contort into a snarl but managed to shift it to one of concern. "He told me not to give it away to anyone. I'll be in trouble if he finds out I gave it to you." *Not to mention I can't.* The pieces sealed themselves once they were put in. They couldn't be removed until the wearer died, or they were torn out. Hence why Ansom was furious when Caiden put one on him when they were young. The king had only laughed, seeing that the young prince had chosen to keep one for himself and give the other to his servant. He usually tried not to draw attention to it, having grown out his hair to keep it covered, but with the man currently leaning over him, it was proving a futile effort.

Evander didn't like Luten. Luten didn't like him. It was a mutual hatred. Ansom had hired the tutor about a month ago, and for some reason the fool thought that this meant he was somehow allowed to order him around, which was not at all the case. Evander only answered to Caiden. Even then, he stood as Caiden's equal in all but the court affairs, and he could tell the prince 'no'.

Luten, being foreign, didn't seem to understand that. If anything, Evander could order Luten around, but the stubborn windbag only answered to Ansom, or the King, and Evander didn't want to involve the knights unless it was necessary. He'd never had to assert his authority to that extent, and while it was well within his rights to have the moron escorted from the grounds, he didn't want the retaliation from Ansom.

"I'm telling you to give it here. The Innektoh Kir are a piece of the royal treasury and as a magic artifact even one of the pair does not belong on a *servant.*" The man glared. "You may be one of the Vladimir clan, but do not expect me to bow to your every whim. You are still a child. That, and as someone hired by Ansom, you have no grounds to refuse my orders."

*He would use the full name for them. Pathetic.* Evander caught himself short of snarling at the Tutor. Somehow, his being called a child despite being twenty-one years of age annoyed him even more. *That's not how this works.* A messenger ran across the courtyard. "Ah! Prince Caiden!" he yelled.

The tutor whirled around, catching sight of the messenger's cloak as the boy entered a building. "Your Highness!" the man screeched, sprinting after the poor, poor messenger who was about to get an earful.

As soon as the tutor was through the door, the branches above Evander rustled and a figure jumped down from the tree he'd been leaning against.

"Nice job, Eva!" the prince laughed as he pulled the servant to his feet and started running with a firm grip around his wrist.

"Your Highness, you really need to stop skipping your lessons." *At least understand that it makes* my *life difficult.* Even so, he ran alongside the prince, allowing the man to lead the way in their escape.

"Oh, don't be a spoilsport! Good morning, Sir Michael!" The pair dodged through the training yard and the knight was too slow to grab them on their way by.

"Your Highness, get back here— Braden!" the knight roared.

Caiden let go of Evander's hand, darting to the right of the burly man that stepped in their way while Evander spun to his left. They met on the other side of the soldier and Caiden once again grabbed him as they continued running.

"Sorry, Sir Michael!" Evander yelled over his shoulder as he was dragged into the castle.

They ran through the halls, scattering maids and servants as they went, until finally the prince stopped, collapsing against the kitchen counter in laughter.

Evander bent double, waiting patiently until it would seem acceptable for his breath to be back before straightening up again.

"Heh… we… we gave him a good run," Caiden panted, still chuckling.

*Idiot.* "You really need to stop skipping your lessons."

"Oh, hush. It's not like they're all that important anyways."

"Really?" Evander raised an eyebrow at the man and pulled a small, leather bound book from his inner pocket. He flipped it open and made a show of looking over the page. "Because today you have a tea party with Her Highness, Princess Marie, and she expects you to dance with her."

Caiden visibly paled. "When was that decided?"

"During your last dance lesson. Which you skipped."

Caiden slouched and grumbled. "I hate dancing, I'm awful at it."

Evander sighed and snapped his book closed, tucking it away. "Your Highness, dancing is an integral part of any and all social outings which, may I remind you, will be increasing after your coronation." He could see the cook grinning out of the corner of his eye and a few of her helpers were biting their cheeks to keep from chuckling.

Caiden slouched further and grumbled, a light blush gracing his fair skin. "Y'know, you sure can lecture. You might give Luten a run."

Evander took a breath but forced himself not to sigh again as he pinched the bridge of his nose. "My apologies, Your Highness," *you irresponsible, selfish, moronic, pathetic excuse for a prince,* "however, Princess Marie will be very disappointed if she isn't able to show you her newfound skill at dancing. Personally, I'd rather not see the young princess cry."

Caiden flinched and groaned. "Fine. When's the tea party?"

Evander glanced out the window. "We still have three hours. Enough time to teach you a simple waltz and have you bathed and ready."

"And who's gonna teach me? Hmm?" Caiden smirked at him and Evander caught himself just short of glaring. Instead, he schooled his features into an expression of confusion.

"Governess Liza—"

"Will probably tan both of our hides before sending us to Father. Or Ansom."

Evander bit the inside of his cheek. "You can't skip the party."

"No, no, I was just thinking, even if I skip my lessons, you usually don't," the prince grinned.

"You want *me* to teach you?" Evander demanded, irritably.

"You can, can't you?"

"Well yes, but—"

"Then it's decided." Caiden nodded to himself, grabbing his arm again as he began walking.

Evander seethed, shooting a glare at the cook who was now openly snickering at him. Karen simply shook her head and went back to her work. He glowered at the prince's back for a moment before he sighed and rearranged his demeanor into a pliable one.

*Better to just get it over with.*

He allowed himself to be dragged to one of the large open rooms where they wouldn't be disturbed, then an idea occurred to him.

"Your Highness?" he asked as Caiden discarded his heavier outerwear. He followed suit, sliding out of his jacket and folding it neatly to the side before picking up Caiden's and doing the same.

The prince made a questioning noise in the back of his throat, raising an eyebrow, as he stood in the middle of the open space, waiting for him.

"You skipped your history lessons earlier, didn't you?" Evander stood in front of him, poking and prodding until the prince was standing straight and tall with his arms held open. It drew attention to his stature. Caiden was taller than him by a good two inches, his shoulders broader, though he didn't have a knight's build. He assumed all of the prince's running away from his classes lent a hand towards keeping him fit. Evander himself had a narrower build, lean, and his strength wasn't noticeable at a glance.

Caiden gave him a suspicious look. "Yes?" he said slowly with a questioning tone.

"Brilliant, Sire. Then we shall multitask." Evander positioned them in the proper stances to mimic a proper dance. Close enough to be involved with each other while never touching bodily, save for their hands. Appropriate for a short dance with a young woman with whom you were related.

Caiden groaned. "C'mon, Eva. Just dancing is enough—"

"You will be reciting the history of Kallenport. Begin with location and origin." Evander ignored him, "Left foot first, three step rhythm, one hand under my arm, three fingers to back, the other held here." He extended his left arm, grabbing Caiden's wrist and turning his hand palm-upwards before placing his own hand lightly above the Prince's. "Forward with the left, bring the right up and over, bring feet together, shift weight. Right foot back, left back and over, bring feet together. Repeat."

Caiden was at least quick to follow his spoken orders, assuming the proper position without too much correction on Evander's part.

"Uh, warm-water port, bordered by mountains to the east and to the south. Thanks to that, it was highly sought after during the original wars some four hundred years ago," Caiden began as Evander pulled him into the first few steps. He was awkward, watching their feet and trying to predict how Evander was going to move.

"And the founders?" Evander prompted, pausing to allow Caiden to regain his balance and slowing his movements so the other had the chance to at least pretend to lead properly.

"Vladimir and Kailyn. Twins. Vladimir was the strategist while Kailyn was the more charismatic— sorry," Caiden cut himself off, trodding on Evander's foot before he could move out of the way.

The servant brushed it off. "And?"

"And between the two of them, they managed to take the land for their own though it was a bloody battle.

Vladimir gave Kailyn the crown, and instead became something like the King's advisor and protector. That was where your family got its name." Caiden grinned briefly, trying to drag Evander off topic.

"Not family, but yes. Those trained in a particular style are considered a part of the 'Vladimir clan,'" Evander supplemented, refusing to abandon the history lesson to go into the clan's origins. "There you have the basic steps. Try to lead."

Caiden was quiet as he focused on leading them through the simple dance, still watching their feet.

"Eyes up. Either over your partner's shoulder or their face," Evander commanded, and Caiden's head shot up, immediately stepping on Evander's toes and dropping his eyes back down.

Evander bit back a sigh and stopped them, "Look up."

Caiden did.

"Back in position. Light steps. I move back as you move forward. One, two, three, in a round. Our feet aren't going to be on the same path. Mine are slightly to the side of yours. Try again without looking." The problem was that Caiden was overly concerned with stepping on him, compensating even though there was no need to.

Evander let him focus on just the steps for a round before prompting him again. "And how did Kallenport manage to avoid civil war with twins as their leaders?"

"Vladimir swore to never have children," Caiden replied. He was finding the rhythm and Evander gave up his control of their pace, letting the other lead. "So there wouldn't be a war over succession."

"Alright." Evander hummed for a moment, mulling over the information that Caiden could have missed. Or he could just annoy him. Petty revenge and all that. "And the laws forbidding magic?" It would have been a few generations down the line but still fell within the timeframe of history that would have been reviewed in the prince's previous lesson.

Caiden's jaw clenched and his stride shortened, causing a momentary hiccup in their steps. "What about it?"

Evander ignored the prince's clear temper. He knew Caiden wanted to change the laws and that he hated their existence with every fiber of his being. It was possibly the man's only redeeming feature.

"Why do we have them?"

"Because when there was famine and disease and everyone was suffering, some of those who could use magic decided to use it to steal and murder and cause chaos wherever they went. They rallied followers and tried to overthrow the King."

"The result?" he pushed the subject further, clearly goading the other.

"They were crushed. All were executed. Magic became something hated and illegal." Caiden's voice was cold and sharp, his fingers curling painfully around Evander's.

"The punishment?"

Caiden glared at him, but his steps didn't falter as he focused more on the conversation than on his movements. "Death."

"Very good, Sir." Evander gave a nod. "And since then, Kallenport has celebrated a long period of peace. Now, if you'd like to add a bit of flare to the dance, you may release one of the lady's hands and shorten your step."

Caiden did so and Evander let himself spin outwards, their hands still conjoined, but before he could continue his explanation, Caiden gave a tug on his arm and spun him back where he lost his balance and the damn prince had the nerve to let him lean back precariously before bringing him back up to stand annoying close.

Evander gave him an irritated look that he didn't bother to hide. "That, Your Highness, is for courting. Not for your sister." The idiot only laughed.

--†--

"Oh!" the little girl gasped in joyous wonder, and Evander smiled at how she restrained herself from running up to the table that had been set up in the garden. He walked behind Caiden, along with Marie's servant, as the prince led his sister down the path.

"Eva, you really outdid yourself. Katie, you'll be just as good as Eva someday!" the princess chattered excitedly, trying to sound older than she was.

The princess had turned nine the past spring, beginning her court training in earnest. Evander watched as Kaitlyn meekly ducked her head, though he could see her hands curl into fists. He wondered if he had been so obvious in his hatred of Caiden at her age. She'd learn though. After all, she'd been assigned to the princess at the age of seven.

Kaitlyn was considered a prodigy in their group, entrusted with the task a year earlier than most. The girl that had been assigned to the princess originally had been deemed well-suited and while she was more than capable, Kaitlyn had challenged her for the position. That challenge came in the form of single combat and Kaitlyn was introduced as Marie's servant the next month.

Evander hadn't agreed with the outcome. The original choice was a calm, level-headed, and fundamentally kind girl; Lissa was her name. All members of the Vladimir clan had some form of magic, though it was a closely guarded secret. In the area, magic most commonly came in the form of abilities, an increase of strength or a very specific talent or power. Lissa's ability had been a simple one — she could cause light to emit from her body. Usually she used it in her palm to illuminate a space, but Evander had once faced her in a spar. He hadn't been nice about it. After all, it was an evaluation. Even so, she'd managed to dodge him, get close to his face, and he'd suddenly found himself blinded by a bright flash.

In the end, he'd won simply because he had the experience that she didn't and the fact that he was older and outweighed her. Hence, she'd been accepted as a candidate for the Princess' Guardian. He'd liked her; she was sweet. Then Kaitlyn came along, and of course with her combat-oriented ability she'd won. Evander was still angry over the outcome. Lissa had suffered a concussion and several broken bones during what should have been a safe match. She'd had to withdraw and if Evander was correct, she'd become an aide in the library along with her brother who had a similar ability even though he didn't have her control.

"You really outdid yourself," Kaitlyn pitched her voice in a mocking whine. She flashed a sneer in his direction before muttering sullenly, "I'd think you were more suited to being a butler,"

Evander glanced at her from the corner of his eye as the royal siblings reached the table. He'd only arranged for it to happen. He'd called for the princess' favorite cakes and candies to be served with her preferred tea. He'd organized the servants to set up the table in the garden clothed in a pale yellow to complement the princess' favorite dress which, sure enough, she'd worn. The pink flowers that accented the table and the three musicians had been easy enough to gather and the gardener had been overjoyed to find that the princess wanted to hold her little tea party amongst his handiwork.

"It was simple enough. You'll learn too, eventually."

"We'll see," she huffed.

Evander frowned at the way that she'd said that. He didn't reply, taking his place off to the side and glancing around, gesturing for the musicians to start a soft background melody. Something didn't feel right. He turned to look around while Caiden pulled out his sister's chair and waited for her to settle before taking his own seat.

The only people in the garden were the royal siblings, the musicians, Kaitlyn, and himself.

"I'm so glad you could meet with me. I feel like I never get to see you anymore," Marie said as Caiden relaxed. She glanced around, and Evander realized that there was no servant to pour the tea.

He stepped forward with a bow. "I beg your pardon, Your Highness." He didn't wait for permission as he plucked a petal from one of the flowers and gently removed the teapot's lid. He dipped the petal into the tea and waited for a moment before removing it again. The pink had turned blue where it had touched the liquid. Even as he watched, spots began to appear on the petal, turning green then grey as the poison ate at it.

"I apologize, Your Highness, but would you mind if I remade the tea? I think you would find it unsuitable." He looked to Caiden without any outward sign of stress though he tilted his hand so while Marie couldn't see the decaying petal, the prince could.

The princess looked up at him, confused, but Caiden understood. "Ah, why don't you show me how well you've learned to dance? I don't think I can imagine it without you stepping on my toes," the prince teased.

Marie took the bait, standing with a huff and demanding that he take her to the clear area in front of the musicians. With the princess distracted, Evander took the entire tea set and prepared to walk back to the kitchens.

He turned to Kaitlyn, about to ask her to keep an eye on them, but he fell silent at the look of frustration on her face. It was gone in a moment, but he was sure that he'd seen it. He decided against asking her to do anything, starting down the path. As soon as he was within sight of a guard, he waved the man over.

"What can I do for you, Evander?" the soldier asked.

"The tea for the princess's party was poisoned. Go watch them while I remake it."

"Poisoned? Has the king been informed?" The guard was already glancing over to where the royal siblings were dancing.

"No. I will give Ansom a report once I see the prince to his afternoon studies. For now, just make sure nothing else happens."

"Yes, Sir." The man saluted but hesitated. "Isn't Miss Kaitlyn already informed and on guard?"

Evander gave him a narrow-eyed look and the man shifted uncomfortably.

"Er... I'll just make sure nothing happens, right?"

"That will be all."

The soldier saluted again and headed off towards the venue while Evander continued on his way at a brisk pace. A servant saw him coming and met him on the path, accepting the tray that Evander handed him.

"Poisoned. Take care to use a new bucket and dump the water in the barrel to be sent to a purifier."

"Yes, Sir." The servant was quick to scuttle back into the castle, and the cook met him at the door.

"Another one?" she asked, already handing him another tray.

"Yeah. This will be the third attempt this month that has gotten so close."

The cook snorted her amusement. "Close. You always catch it as soon as it gets anywhere near Caiden." She picked the kettle up off the stove and filled the teapot, setting it on his tray as soon as she was finished.

"Have you caught the one responsible?" she asked as he turned to leave.

"I'm sure I will in the next few minutes. They would have stayed close to watch."

"Good luck."

Evander gave her a nod and headed back down the path.

The only reason he noticed the body was the bird that was circling. He set the tray down to the side and wandered closer, finding the serving girl that should have been attending to the royal siblings. She'd been strangled.

The scuff of feet on stone, rustle of branches, thud of footfalls on the grass. Evander shifted to the side in time to avoid being grabbed. He easily danced out of the way and stood facing the would-be assassin.

The man was too thin, filthy, with a crazed light shining in his eyes as he grinned a gap-toothed smile. "So close. If not for you theys be dead. All would be well. Theys be dead 'nd I'd be paid and all'd be well," he muttered mostly to himself, curled and fidgeting as he eyed Evander.

The servant shifted back a step and slid a knife from the sheath on his forearm into his hand. He wasn't too concerned for his own safety. This man was clearly under the influence of some kind of drug. He'd most likely been hired from the slums of the lower city and given the poison. Which meant there were bribed guards to deal with. Or dead ones. Either that or there was a noble or someone influential trying to kill the heirs.

"Who hired you?" he asked calmly.

"I'm not apposed to tell you tha'." The man tilted his head. "I'm apposed to ge' ridda anyone in my way." He pulled a rusted blade from a makeshift sheath at his side and swung wildly at him.

Evander leaned out of the way, quickly stepping towards the man and swinging out with his elbow. The guy was faster than he'd originally thought, managing to pull away from the blow to his temple. He threw himself backwards as the man slashed at him.

"Eva?"

Evander flinched as Caiden's voice rang out. That bastard always did have an uncanny ability to know when he was unwanted.

"Stay back, Your Highness!" He dodged, trying to think of how to end it quickly without revealing the true extent of his combative experience. As the prince's bodyguard, he was expected to be trained, but the style he used was closer to a trained killer's than a soldier's. It was certainly not something he needed Caiden questioning him about.

Instead of following after him, his opponent switched targets. The man charged at Caiden. The prince frantically looked around for a weapon but there was nothing in reach.

*Fool,* Evander mentally cursed and sprinted forward, diving and anchoring his hands on the path as his legs swung out. The man tripped and tangled with him. In close proximity, Evander managed to disarm him, throwing the blade away though the man managed to land several blows while he did so.

Finally, Evander trapped him, the assassin's arm tight in his grip and his legs applying pressure to the man's neck, choking him. The assassin kicked and thrashed but eventually fell still as Evander only tightened his hold.

He waited a moment, making sure it was safe before he kicked the unconscious man away, slowly getting back to his feet. He'd skinned the heels of his hands on the rough stone of the pathway, the sting a minor irritation as he dusted himself off.

"Are you alright, Your Highness?" he asked slowly, painting a concerned expression over his features.

"Er, yes, I'm fine. Are you...?"

"Oh, I'm alright." He forced a smile, going to pick up the tea tray. "I was trained to protect you after all."

"Are you sure you shouldn't go see the Physician?"

"Your Highness, I assure you, I'm fine. Besides, the princess will be worried. Speaking of which, what are you doing here?"

"You were taking a while and Marie was starting to worry. I offered to find you." He mumbled almost as an afterthought, "swear, she likes you more than me."

"Why didn't you send the guard instead?"

"I left him to protect the ladies."

"So, you came, unarmed?" Evander was careful to keep his tone light but internally he was seething at the stupidity.

The prince glared. "How was I supposed to know you were being attacked? Besides that, what would you have done if I hadn't come along?" he snapped.

*I would have been fine. In fact, I would have been finished with it much faster had you not interrupted.* "I apologize, Your Highness. I meant no disrespect. I am simply concerned for your safety." He forcefully kept his tone civil.

Caiden narrowed his eyes at him. "Fine. C'mon. Before Marie tries to come after us herself," he muttered and turned his back on the servant.

Oh, how Evander longed to sink a blade into that arrogant brat. He had the kingdom at his beck and call, unlimited power at his fingertips, yet he insisted on acting like an irresponsible, spoiled child. He took a deep breath and reigned in his temper. *All good things to those who wait.*

He followed after Caiden, smiling at the princess as she ran up to him.

"Eva, are you alright? Brother said to wait, but I was worried."

"He's fine, Marie. He just tripped on his way there," Caiden interjected, his tone a bit harsher than necessary.

"Are you alright?" Her hand was light on his arm, large, green-hued eyes staring up at him with worry.

He smiled at her. "I am sorry that I worried you, Princess. Though, I am honored that I am worth your concern."

She gave him a tiny little smile, a blush staining her face as she followed Caiden back to the table. He set the tray down and distributed the cups, easily pouring out the tea and serving a few of the cakes.

He chuckled as she chided Caiden's lack of preparation. 'How are you supposed to help Eva when you didn't even bring a knife?' Meaning she had figured it out. She had probably seen the scuff marks on his hands while he set out her drink.

She was a sweet kid. Intelligent for her age and quick witted. She would make an excellent Queen should Caiden die before securing the succession. She was also exceedingly compassionate without being overly trusting. He smiled to himself as he turned to the soldier who was waiting off to the side.

"Did you restrain the man?" he asked.

"Yes, he is being taken to the dungeon to be interrogated. I also had Susan's body removed."

"Good. I'll give a report to Ansom once I see the prince safely to his afternoon lectures."

The guard bowed in acknowledgment. "Would you like me to stay?"

"Within earshot, yes, but an armed guard would detract from the illusion that they are perfectly safe here. I'd like them to relax, at least while they are together." He looked over at the pair, watching Marie giggle at Caiden who was talking animatedly.

The guard grinned. "You are very kind to arrange this. The maids were at their wits' ends with the princess' tantrums."

"It was nothing." He waved off the compliment. "I merely did what was necessary."

The guard bowed again. "Of course, Sir. Just call if you need anything."

Evander watched the man leave and returned to his post in the background, keeping an eye on the proceedings and only stepping forward to refill cups or plates as needed.

Marie was ten years younger than Caiden and the prince used to play with her instead of attending his lessons. However, since she'd come of age, the time they spent together was nearly nonexistent save for suppers, since the Queen insisted on having a 'family meal'. Having served there as well, Evander knew that even those were no longer a source of joy for the royal children.

The king was a kind and gentle man, although frivolous in some ways. The Queen was severe and clearly uninterested in her political marriage. In fact, while the king treated Marie as his daughter, doting on her and loving her unconditionally, she was not his. She looked enough like him that there were no harmful rumors and Marie herself was unaware of her own illegitimacy. However, Caiden knew, as did Evander. While Caiden never treated the girl any differently and loved her as though she were his full blood relation, he chose to show his opinion of his mother's affairs by ignoring the woman.

The Queen responded by putting more pressure on him as the heir and the dinners that were once full of idle chatter and laughter now were battles filled with barbed comments and thinly veiled insults between mother and son. Marie, stuck in the middle with no knowledge as to the reasons behind them, only saw the conflict and the strain it was putting on her father who was trying to hold it together.

Understandably, the princess had started throwing tantrums, insisting that Caiden come to see her and refusing to take part in her lessons until he did. Evander had solved the problem by bribing her with this tea party and the promise that she'd have her brother all to herself for a few hours. He also left her with the manipulative suggestion that she could impress him with all of her new knowledge if she paid attention to her lessons. It had worked, if her chatter about etiquette was anything to go by.

"As I said, butler would suit you much better," Kaitlyn growled.

"It is a part of our official jobs," he muttered back.

The girl scoffed. "They're right. You are pathetically soft."

He barely held back the urge to punch her in the mouth- prodigy or not, she was an eleven-year-old girl. "Well, if you fail at your official job, it won't matter how good you are at killing, you'll fail the clan either way. Then we'll see who's worth more."

That certainly shut her up. He could practically feel the rage radiating off of her. As satisfying as it was, Evander cursed himself for it. She was not someone who he wanted against him and she was currently Ansom's favorite. He had no doubt that if the girl had been born a male he would have been disposed of long ago and replaced.

The time passed uneventfully, and Evander was relieved when Caiden saw Marie to her room and was too tired to run from his classes.

"You won't be joining me?" the prince asked, surprised, when Evander made to leave him with his tutor.

"No, I have to give my report to Ansom. I will return shortly."

"Oh, okay then. Don't envy you that." Caiden gave him a lazy wave as he turned to greet his teacher.

Evander bowed, relieved that the prince wasn't trying to weasel his way out of his lesson. However, knowing Caiden, if he wasn't quick, the man would disappear for the rest of the day.

He quickly made his way through the castle, taking side passages and little-used halls to get to the entrance of the King's study, where the head of the Vladimir clan could usually be found.

He nodded to the guards, waiting as one of them knocked on the door. A few moments later, Ansom answered. His black hair was showing streaks of grey, the only sign of the man's age as far as Evander knew. He wasn't fooled. The man was still as strong as ever, his shrewd gaze raking over Evander's form with barely contained loathing.

"Evander." It was a statement, not a question, as though he was already expected.

It made Evander wince.

Ansom strode past him and Evander silently followed him down the hall, around the corner where a decorative statue stood surrounded by stained glass windows. He came to a stop in front of it and waited, not even bothering to take his eyes from the stone.

Evander took it as his cue and stepped forward, putting his shoulder to the stone and pushing hard, having to throw almost his entire weight into the task. The statue slid back with a slight grating sound to reveal a set of stairs. He stood aside as Ansom descended then followed, pausing to pull the statue forward until he could feel the indent in the base. Then he ducked his head down and braced his body against the stairs to push the heavy stone back into place.

He remembered a time when he used to struggle to open and close this particular passage. It would make his arms ache and many times he'd have to resort to alternative methods of closing it. Now, it was only a slight strain.

He followed the dark passage, pausing at the bottom of the narrow staircase. He listened for a moment, trying to determine which way Ansom had gone. He knew where the man was most likely to go but he was not entirely sure, so he was left trying to follow the man by sound.

Ansom didn't make it easy. Then again, he had no reason to. Evander wasn't a child and like all the others in the Vladimir clan, he had been trained since he could walk, tutored from the moment he could form cohesive thoughts. He could detect only the slightest noise, the rustling of clothing.

The Inner Castle, as they called it, was a narrow and winding labyrinth. Built beneath the floors and between the walls of the castle itself. It was the Vladimir clan's closely guarded secret. He passed peepholes and hidden doorways, listening in passing to the low chatter of diplomats, nobles, and servants alike.

It took him a few minutes before he arrived at a large, soundproofed, multipurpose room. Training equipment littered the room, cots around the edges, tables, boards, and a large sparring circle drawn with chalk in the middle.

Ansom stood in the center of the circle, slowly spinning a throwing knife in his hand. He glared when Evander walked in.

"You took three minutes." The condescending sneer made it clear that that was unacceptable.

"Yes, Master." Evander bowed his head, but he never took his eyes off of the man.

"Do you understand just how replaceable you are? You have the Prince's trust and, currently, it would require too much effort to shift his affections to someone else. However, you yourself are worthless outside of your role. Is that clear?"

"Yes, Master. You have made that abundantly clear." He couldn't stop the comment and he swallowed the yelp of pain that tried to escape as a dagger slid across his cheek. He felt the warmth of blood start to pool and slide over his skin. He didn't move to stop it, seeing as it would only enrage the man further.

"Yet, for some reason, you seem to be painfully unaware. Or perhaps you are simply that stupid."

Evander stayed silent, the pain in his cheek doing a fine job of reminding him just how little he meant to the clan. Not that they ever really let him forget.

"Well? I expect you to answer when spoken to. Or have you truly become nothing more than a mere servant?"

"I beg your pardon, Master, perhaps I have adjusted too well to the role that you've given me." This time the dagger pierced his hand, punching through the limb and into his thigh since his arms had been at his sides. It had been perfectly aimed as Ansom's ability activated, not damaging anything but causing enough pain to leave him breathless.

Impeccable Aim. Whether it was daggers, arrows, rocks, silverware, anything that the man threw with the intent of hitting always hit. Always. Exactly as he wanted them to. If he didn't hit you, then that only meant that he didn't want to hit you.

Evander didn't dare to move. Didn't dare to flinch. Show no weakness; to do so would only give the man another excuse to ridicule him.

Ansom snarled, stalking over to him and ripping the dagger out. "Impertinent, child. What did you come to report?"

"An assassination attempt on the royal children. We have the perpetrator in custody; however I have reason to believe that there is someone within the castle who is responsible for it." His voice was even and steady as he tried to block out the pain in his hand and leg.

"Oh? And what makes you think that?" Ansom's tone was guarded as he circled him. It was either a test, or he already knew something.

"The assassin was ill-suited to the job and dispensable. However, he was distinctive. He wouldn't have gotten past the guards without some sort of help. The poison itself is a rare variety, nothing he would have procured himself. I am under the impression that it is a visiting noble or..." he trailed off for a moment but quickly finished the sentence before Ansom could demand to know what he was implying. "Or a spy acting as a servant."

*There's no way it could be one of us.* Evander mentally disregarded his own gut feeling. *An ambassador or one of the nobles would have more to gain than one of the clan.*

He held still as a dagger's blade pressed beneath his chin, forcing him to bare his throat to avoid getting cut.

"That's an awful lot of assumptions. You know how I hate those."

"You already have the reports, don't you? I am simply interpreting based on the information I have. Given time, I could give you a solid theory if not a culprit. However, if you already know everything then I see no reason—"

He saw the flash of rage in the man's eyes just before the dagger withdrew from his throat, the pommel slamming into the side of his face with startling speed. He stumbled, his legs giving out as his head spun from the blow.

"You dare to question me?"

Evander looked up at Ansom as the man stood over him, murder a live and dancing emotion writhing over his features. He felt his blood run cold at the sight.

"You." Ansom's foot braced against his shoulder and Evander didn't dare to resist as the man forced him onto his back. "Your life is worthless. As far as I am concerned, you are a waste of my resources."

The man's weight settled painfully atop his shoulder, crushing the joint.

"I did not question you, Master, only your intentions. If I do not return to my duties, the prince will likely slip away from me. If you already have the information, then I apologize for wasting your time." He let his hands rest even with his shoulders, palms up, unarmed, defenseless.

He knew the man well. He knew that despite his hatred of him, he would never kill him this way. No, he'd let him fight. He'd let him fight and hope. Then watch that hope turn to desperation. Then to despair. Then, and only then, would he kill him.

Ansom growled, pressing harder against his shoulder, the joint straining against the weight of the man, then suddenly he backed off.

"Your punishment will be dealt later. Get out of my sight."

Evander slowly sat up, cradling his injured hand in an attempt to staunch the bleeding. He got to his feet, his leg aching where the dagger had pierced his skin and limped down one of the halls that branched off of the room.

As soon as he was out of sight, he lengthened his stride, pulling a handkerchief to wrap around his hand and ignoring the pain in his thigh. Ansom was growing restless. Any question was treated as an act of disobedience. All disobedience was treated with brutal, efficient punishment. You either fell in line, or you died.

It hadn't been that way until recently. Ansom hadn't seemed to care what his people did so long as they did their jobs. Then, slowly but surely, he tightened his hold on all of them and by then it was too late to question him. He hadn't led them astray yet at least. Whatever was bothering the man had to be on a grand scale to make him this stressed.

Evander tried to think over the last few months, identifying what could have triggered the sudden change. His own treatment hadn't changed much, but Ansom had never been so physically violent with him before. Emotionally abusive? Yes, absolutely. If he weren't so stubborn and prideful in his own way then he actually feared for what might have become of him. Sure, he had scars from the few times that he'd caught Ansom in the wrong mood, but this type of physical damage had been consistent only for the past two weeks or so.

To his knowledge, nothing had changed save for the loss of a few members. One to a chronic illness, another to a hunting accident, and the last to old age. Even that wasn't that rare. Their position as members of the Vladimir clan came with a certain amount of risk.

Evander sighed and abandoned that line of thought for the moment.

The Vladimir clan had served the royal family since the kingdom's foundation. Over the years, they began to rule from the shadows, subtly manipulating the Kings and heirs to keep the kingdom prosperous. If the king was found unsuited and his heir incompetent, then the clan would take over. They had become assassins alongside their duties as bodyguards and servants. It had only happened once in their history that their alternate role needed fulfilled. A king had planned to give over his crown to a neighboring kingdom, a desperate act founded by a famine that had already taken thousands of lives. His daughter had only been three and incapable of taking the throne, so the clan head of the time assassinated his charge. With the king dead, as per the kingdom's laws, with the Queen as head consul, the head of the Vladimir clan became Regent until the princess was old enough to take over.

There were requirements in place for the royalty, of course. Tactical ability, control over emotion, combat ability, wisdom, and the ability to always put the kingdom first. Some were replaceable in favor of having a king who was easily manipulated. Caiden was none of the above and he was too stubborn to blindly follow orders.

It didn't bother Evander. He had a hatred for the prince that was hard to explain in its intensity. However, the same idiot was quite literally the only reason he was alive. Yes, he had been the best of the best, but his ability had been late to bloom. When he'd been assigned to the position, no one had known what he would become. Yet when his ability finally manifested, he suddenly dropped to the very bottom.

Shadow Dancer, they called him. He could move from one shadow to the next as though he'd stepped through a doorway. It came with too many limitations. The shadow had to be big enough to fit through, he had to have a direct line of sight to his exit point, there had to be shadows in the first place, and it made him violently ill when he used it. It became useless. The only upside was that it was easy to hide.

Well, that's how it started at least. They deemed him worthless, they stopped testing him. He was left to his own devices as far as his ability was concerned and while it may have been called a useless failure of a talent, he found it to his liking. By the time the ability had grown and his control of it had strengthened, it had already become obvious that he was hated. It became his own little secret, a way to escape if he ever needed it.

"Dear Gods! What in the world happened to you?"

He blinked at the cook as he stepped out of the dry cellar where an entrance to the Inner Castle was secreted away.

"Eh," he replied slowly, turning his head so she could see the wound on his cheek and held up his hand.

She was one of them, the only healing ability in the clan. Karen tisked and shoved him none too gently back into the pantry, her ability activating as she grabbed his chin, then his hand, running her fingers over his leg before abruptly turning away again.

From the Brink was the ability to heal the wounds she touched. However, they had to be severe for it to work. A fractured bone would have to be broken before she could fix it, and open bloody wounds seemed to be the only surface wounds affected. Considering that anything less was easily recovered from, it was a fairly useful ability.

She marched over to the sinks and threw a damp towel at him, watching him wipe the blood and dirt away from his skin.

"I can't fix bruises," she huffed at him as she violently kneaded her dough.

"I know. Thanks for the help." He gave the woman a genuine smile. For as gruff as she was, she was one of the few that didn't want him dead, so he supposed that was enough reason for him to like her. "Do you have any idea what's going on?" he asked, leaning against her counter.

"No clue. Now get out before they think I like you." She gave him a pointed look and a small playful grin as she shooed him away.

He grinned, taking his leave to go and find where that damn Prince had gone.

# Chapter Two
Month of the Griffin 10, 421 HE

"Get up, Evander."

Evander struggled to his knees, his head still spinning as he shoved himself back to his feet. He swayed, and the room seemed to tilt before he managed to regain his balance.

Kaitlyn grinned at him from across the sparring ring, bloodlust clear on her face. Ansom stood to the side along with the rest of the clan's members, save for those who had other duties.

"Again. This time, try to give her at least a small challenge," Ansom sighed. Evander grit his teeth, taking a deep breath to try and right himself.

Kaitlyn bounced on the balls of her feet, continuously moving. Her ability was annoying to fight.

Catlike Reflexes. She had the uncanny ability to dodge, but it also made her faster, more flexible than most humans. It made her near impossible to hit and made all of her blows hurt like hell.

His limbs trembled with fatigue, and he didn't want to use his ability. He was stuck facing her as he was. She darted forward, and he lost sight of her for a second as she closed the distance. He used to be the best. He steeled his spine and let loose his temper.

He could feel her presence to his right. Kaitlyn preferred quick jabs to vulnerable places, so she would be in close quarters. She had to stay still for a least a few moments to deliver the blow. Her aim would most likely be for his kidney if she was coming at him from the side. Evander took a quick step towards her, reaching out and absorbing the blow. It made him want to puke but he grinned as his hand caught her neck.

Instead of throwing her away from him, he pulled her in, hooking his heel around her ankles and pulling her feet out from under her as he slammed her into the floor. She was a small thing; he found he could easily lift her like she was nothing. She gasped and thrashed, clawing at his arm and face, trying to get her legs up high enough to kick him or at least find purchase to throw him off. He wouldn't allow it. He picked her up and slammed her down again, watching with savage glee as her head hit the floor. She faltered for a moment, frothing at the mouth in her struggle to breathe. She finally switched her aim, her fist connecting with his leg, just an inch from his groin. He tightened his grip as she struggled. To her credit, she never stopped trying to get out of his hold.

Finally, he gave in to the urge he'd had since that afternoon and punched her in the face. She stopped struggling, slapping his thigh in a sign of yielding. He let her go, watching her cough and curl in on herself.

Coming down from the bloodlust, he felt bad. He was nearly twice her age after all, larger in both height and weight. He got to his feet and offered a hand to her. His reward was a kick to the groin. He reflexively hunched over, her heel meeting his temple in a blinding flash of pain.

He tumbled to the ground, dimly aware that he was twitching, breathless as she repeatedly kicked at him. He curled protectively over himself, letting the blows land as he regained his breath and tried to shove the pain and dizziness away. He was about to retaliate when her kicks finally stopped.

He glanced up at Ansom standing over him, Kaitlyn being dragged away by two of the others. "You disgust me, Evander. Never show compassion. To anyone. They will kill us without a second thought, you should do the same. You have failed. Again."

Evander dropped his gaze to Ansom's feet, rage rising too fast for him to mask it. His fingers curled into fists; teeth clenched. He should have been used to this. He was used to this. The constant stream of abuse, the assault, the harassment. It didn't matter what he did, no matter how hard he tried, how much he struggled, if he won or if he lost, it was always the same. That underhanded attack would have been punished if it had been used against anyone else. Against him, it was applauded.

He waited until Ansom turned away from him before pushing himself into a sitting position. The aches and pains of his body were making themselves violently known now that he wasn't fighting.

A rough hand grabbed his arm and forced him to his feet. "Look at me, Evander." Evander blinked at Karen as the woman forced him into a position of her liking, her fingers tracing over his temple and the worst of his injuries. "Hmm. More bruises. Careful that prince of yours doesn't question you about it."

It was as close as she could get to worrying about him and while he appreciated it, it infuriated him. He pulled away from her, shaking off her hand as he limped to one of the exits. The others kept glancing at him. Most were clearly worried. The clan was tight knit. Their numbers weren't exactly large and while newcomers were always joining or children were being adopted or born, they still shared that one life defining secret of their magic.

It brought everyone closer together. Evander had grown up with them, fought with them, was taught by them. He loved them dearly and he couldn't bring himself to blame them for their continued silence. What Ansom demanded was taken as law. If Ansom saw Evander as a worthless waste of resources then that is how he was meant to be treated... at least in his presence.

It was slow going, making his way through the long, winding passages until he reached the tiny offshoot that would take him to his room. He was stopped several times by others of the clan brave enough to ask if he was alright. It was the same as every other night. He'd smile, say he was fine, and watch them leave though he knew they didn't always believe him.

He slid the false wall closed behind him as he stepped out of the stairway and into his wardrobe. He then gingerly climbed out and let the doors click shut. He stood still for a moment, gathering his breath.

His fist connected with the wooden doors of the wardrobe before he could resist the rage that engulfed him. Pain burst across his knuckles, helping to douse his anger before he could hit it again. He forced himself to focus on that pain, waiting until he was sure his temper was back under control. It would be difficult to explain away a broken piece of furniture. He flexed his hand, relishing the ache that remained after the abuse.

This had been happening for years now. Granted it had only gotten to the point of being downright malicious over the past month as if they were trying to make him run away or just roll over and let himself be killed. He glared at his reddened knuckles. They were in for a rude awakening. He was good at his job. He took pride in it. And one day Ansom would have to step down and Evander would be free to do as he pleased.

*Just a few weeks more.*

Evander let his head fall against the wardrobe doors with a dull *thunk*. He just wanted it to go back to being peaceful. He lightly hit the wardrobe again, not enough to do any damage but even the ache in his hand wasn't enough to fully sate his sudden need to destroy something.

A noise made him look down as a large fluffy cat rubbed against his legs. Purring. Happy to see him despite his tantrum.

"Mira," he cooed at the cat as he picked her up and held her for a moment. "How did you get in here?" He felt his anger finally fade completely as the animal nuzzled his chin.

Evander kissed her head and scratched her neck. He'd found her a few years ago, half drowned after a rainstorm. She was more Karen's cat than his, finding more food and more attention in the kitchen than with Evander. Still, she occasionally slept in his bed and always greeted him if she saw him.

She was a welcome balm to his frayed nerves and often wayward temper. She licked his face, reminding him that he was currently filthy.

One of the luxuries that came with being the Guardian of the Crown Prince was a washtub in his own room. He also had a small stove to keep the room warm in the cold months. It was late; his small window showed the darkness that came in the hour before midnight.

He winced as he put the cat down and forced himself to move to the door, giving a nod to the guards that stood by the prince's room. Both returned the gesture and he could feel them watching him as he made his way to the servant's quarters to fetch water for a short bath. He could tell he wasn't walking properly; he was still aching from Kaitlyn's kick and his head hurt though Karen had fixed the worst of it.

*Is her ability still growing?* he mused as he lifted the two buckets and started to make his way back to his room. He'd only ever known her to heal physical wounds, though he supposed a head injury might count.

He shrugged off the thought. It didn't matter. It's not like her ability was judged on power.

He nodded to the guards and paused, surprised, when one walked over to open his door for him. He raised an eyebrow at the man, the expression returned by a smile.

"Don't think a few steps to the right will get me suspended in the wee hours," the guard gave him a light-hearted wink. The soldier's gaze swept over him, taking in the scuff marks and bruises that showed on his skin. The guards weren't stupid. Yet, it wasn't unusual for the Vladimir clan to have their own training regimen, so their injuries were overlooked. All that mattered was that the members could pass the tests that the knights set for them to prove their capability.

Evander chuckled. "Thank you." He slipped inside and listened to the guard's footsteps as he returned to his post.

Bathing was quick and efficient, scrubbing the dirt from his skin before redressing into something more comfortable to sleep in. He laid down a while after midnight, looking out at the faint silver light that came between midnight and dawn, the moon beginning its slow descent.

He winced as he rolled onto his side, his body still aching.

*There will be bruises tomorrow.* It would be a pain having to try and dodge Caiden's questioning. He sighed and settled beneath the blankets to try and sleep for a few hours.

He was nearly successful. His dozing was startled by the slightest creak of a door opening. He didn't move, didn't give away that he knew someone was there, his hand sliding towards the dagger that he kept beneath the pillow.

Quiet, hesitant footsteps slowly approached his bed and he relaxed. Not an assassin or any of the clan coming to beat him senseless. It was only Caiden.

Evander had noticed this habit early in his service to the prince. The man hated sleeping alone. As a child, he would be easily scared in his large suite. It was the first fight they'd ever had, when Caiden tried to crawl into his bed and Evander had kicked the young prince out with a finality that seemed to stick.

The child received a dog less than a year later and the pup — and later, large hound — could usually be found curled up behind the prince's knees come morning. Something that Evander despised since his hatred of dogs went both ways. The creatures were sensitive to magic users and had been bred for generations to hunt them down. He couldn't even count the number of times he'd almost been bitten. However, the dog kept the prince company and it saved Evander from having to fight with him.

That changed when he was eleven. The prince had been nine at the time and had started attending larger social functions. The stable master back then had been a kind soul. He was a large, well-built man and quite possibly the nicest person Evander had ever met. He'd been the one to give Caiden the pup from his dog's litter and had taught both boys how to properly ride horses since Caiden didn't like the riding instructor.

He was found guilty of having magic. Something simple, an affinity for animals. He could understand their thoughts and feelings. He had been sentenced to death and Caiden had been made to attend the execution. Evander had watched the boy beg and cry, pleading with his father to try and stop it. No one had listened. The child could only stand and watch. Finally, Caiden ran, and Evander was excused to go after him. He was thankful they didn't have to watch the end.

That day, Caiden wouldn't let anyone in to see him. He wouldn't eat, wouldn't speak, and even Evander couldn't get him to unbar his door. Finally, they decided to leave him be. That night, when his door swung open and Evander had looked up to see Caiden hesitating in his doorway, he'd moved over and didn't say a word when the child curled up beside him

Since then, Caiden only occasionally wormed his way into his bed and Evander never commented. Truthfully, it had become a relief. The night of the execution, he'd been unable to sleep, sick with the knowledge that it could have been him. Could have been any of the clan. He still had nightmares about it. Later, he was thankful simply because he knew the clan couldn't do anything to him with the prince present.

Evander dragged himself away from those thoughts as Caiden quietly slid into bed beside him, his back resting against his own. Not a word was spoken but

Evander slept soundly, knowing he was relatively safe for the night.

--†--

## Griffin, 11

When he woke up at dawn, the servant was alone in his bed as per usual. He stretched, wincing at the ache in his muscles. He knew he hadn't imagined Caiden's presence. He also knew that after being snapped at, the prince made sure to go back to his own room before Evander woke.

He dressed himself quickly, his thin, flexible daily armor hidden beneath his clothing, and strapping on several daggers. Evander then dedicated a bit of time to digging through his collection of ointments, salves, and cosmetics, applying a mixture to the ugly spots of discoloration on his visible skin. Satisfied that Caiden wouldn't notice the bruising, he put everything back, rinsed his hands, and finally left his room. He caught a servant girl as he walked down the hall, directing her to drain his bath and thanking her before making his way to the kitchens. The hallways were bustling with servants as they cleaned and stocked, the guards changing shifts, and the nobility yet to rise.

The kitchen was fully functioning. Several of the assistants engaged in preparing various ingredients for use throughout the day. Servants were lining up with bowls to receive their breakfast of porridge. Karen herself was arranging the Royal breakfasts, eggs and sausages sizzling in her pan.

Evander took a tray and gathered the prince's breakfast. Eggs, sausage, a small bowl of berries alongside a sliced apple, and with a second thought he grabbed a sweet bun to add to it. Karen eyed the meal, rearranging a few things before setting a small pot of tea down for him to take. She also handed him a bowl of the servant's porridge, as close as she could get to telling him to eat.

He gave her a grin and took it with him, heading out of the kitchen just as Ansom was walking in. He kept his head down and skirted around him, fully aware that the man was watching him like a hawk. He could hear him snapping an order at Karen who, bless the woman's soul, refused to take orders in her own kitchen and could be heard telling him so.

"I'm down an aide, in case you've forgotten—two now with Susan gone," she snapped, her tone icy and pointed, "So, stand there, be quiet, and wait your damn turn. And stop snapping at everyone just because—"

Evander couldn't hear the rest of the conversation as he turned down the hall. He did fear for Karen with Ansom in his current mood, but the woman was the only healing ability that they had. Ansom wouldn't kill her just for doing her job. Hopefully.

He gave a brisk knock before entering the room, letting his eyes adjust to the dim lighting. He set the breakfast tray down on the small table and busied himself picking up the room before filling the bathtub. Thankfully, the bath in the prince's room had a water pump which spared him the trouble of fetching water.

He lit the small stove that sat in the corner of the bathroom, stirring up the coals before setting a kettle to heat and gathering the hotter coals to place under the metal basin to start warming the tub. Once that was done, he went back to the bedroom and pulled back the curtains.

"Your Highness, it's time to wake."

A muffled grumble came from the lump on the bed that was Caiden.

Evander unceremoniously pulled the blankets off of him. The prince opened a singular eye and glared. Evander ignored him, gathering the clothes and blankets that needed to be sent to wash and laying out an appropriate outfit for the prince to wear.

*Butler indeed,* he silently grumbled as he watched Caiden slowly get out of bed and wander over to the table, sitting heavily. He sniffed at the eggs and sausage, his lip curling in disgust as he pushed the plate away. Evander didn't bother to hide his sigh.

"You should at least try to eat some meat in the morning," he said slowly. He knew that Caiden didn't have a very strong stomach in the mornings and the smell of meat made him queasy. The prince, instead, picked at the fruit and pulled the gruel towards himself with a slight smile.

"Yet you always bring porridge along." He looked down at the sweet bun and smiled, recognizing it as a gesture of comfort since Caiden usually only came to his bed now when he was overcome with nightmares or was unbearably lonely. The dog that had kept the prince company for the past ten years or so had finally passed away a few months prior. While Evander didn't miss the hound and was fairly relieved he didn't have to add 'dodge the teeth' to his morning routine anymore, he knew Caiden missed the creature sorely. In consequence, the prince had been more frequent in his nighttime habits over the past month.

Evander hated that part of him that refused to half ass his job. He was supposed to take care of the prince and judge him. Kill him if necessary, yes, but until that order came he was supposed to take care of the idiot.

"You have an appointment with the tailor at ten," he said, ignoring the comment and keeping his voice soft. "Tutor Luten will be teaching you the proper address to the people for your coronation. There is a meeting with her Highness Princess Eudora..." he trailed off when he realized that the prince was examining him. "Your Highness?"

"Eva, are you hurt?"

Evander blinked at him. "No?" He must have been limping still.

They stared at each other for a few seconds before Caiden looked back to his breakfast. "Eat this for me so I don't have to listen to Karen nag." He shoved the plate of meat and eggs towards him.

Evander recognized that the subject was being purposely dropped as it had been before. After all, it wasn't the first time that he'd come to greet him with new bruises. He hesitated before perching on the edge of the other chair.

"Why Eudora?" Caiden asked once Evander started picking at the sausage.

"It's a political marriage. We have a rather prosperous agreement with Terravinter to the north. Eudora is the second-"

"Yes, yes, the second princess of Terravinter, I know. Isn't she still like... ten?"

"She is fifteen this coming year."

"So, she's fourteen. That totally makes it better." Caiden rolled his eyes.

"Your Highness, it is an extremely beneficial union and you wouldn't be marrying her immediately."

Caiden glared at him. "I'm not marrying a girl I barely know."

"Hence why you'll be having frequent meetings with her starting now."

Caiden's glare turned into a scowl as he set his cup down and pushed away from the table. "Finish that before I'm back," he growled, gesturing at the tray.

Evander glanced over what was left of the breakfast. The prince had left the blueberries out of the bowl of fruit, eggs, sausage, and a third of the tea. It had become routine though they still went through the steps of 'arguing' who would eat what. Caiden would eat his fill and Evander would eat the rest.

He waited until the bathroom door shut before digging into the food, finishing and cleaning up by the time Caiden would be finished washing. He grabbed a towel and stepped into the room as Caiden was stepping out. It was the usual routine. Evander bustled around as Caiden dried himself off then stepped into the breeches that the servant handed him. Then the prince sat and let Evander comb and dry his hair into a semblance of style.

The red locks were as stubborn as always in their resistance. Evander glared, cursing Caiden's hair for the umpteenth time. The prince had a stubborn cowlick at the back of his head that made it nearly impossible to make him look presentable. And it was on *his* head if the prince didn't look presentable. He sighed and gave up on it, about to allow Caiden to put on a shirt when he spotted a small scar on the man's back, just on his shoulder. It looked like a knife wound.

"Your Highness, where did you get this?" He lightly touched the spot and watched the man jump.

"What, that?" Caiden craned his head around to try and see the scar. "I got it a while ago."

Evander frowned, tracing over it again. "Really? Because I do this every morning and I've never noticed it."

Caiden laughed. "Well, you're usually too busy fighting with my hair. Come on, Eva, didn't you say that we had to meet with the tailor?"

Reminded of his schedule, he set the issue aside for later and gathered the dishes. "I will bring the tailor up to fetch you. We can use the mirror room for the fitting."

"Fine," Caiden sighed, pulling his shirt over his head and holding still as Evander straightened the fabric so that it laid properly across his shoulders.

"You should read over the speech again, and Luten left you several pamphlets on public speaking."

Caiden snorted his contempt for the idea. "The written form of what he's about to show me?"

Evander sighed again and repressed the urge to glare. "It will take less time if you would just glance over the material beforehand."

Caiden rolled his eyes and Evander had to make a conscious effort to unclench his fists.

"I'll return shortly." He bowed and headed for the door.

"Take your time."

He caught the door just short of slamming it shut. The prince was infuriating. He huffed out a breath, rolled his neck, and straightened his shoulders. *No sense letting him upset you.* He started off down the hall. Honestly, he didn't understand why the man's attitude annoyed him so much. Perhaps it was simply the repetition. Caiden never seemed to get it through his head that he was a prince and should be more concerned with inheriting the kingdom and not making a fool of himself when he did so. Instead, the prince continued to play around and act like a child even though he was nearly twenty.

The tailor would be in the courtyard if he was on time. It was strangely quiet in the castle and he couldn't quite get rid of the feeling that something wasn't right. There was a princess arriving and yet there wasn't any of the usual chaos that went along with that.

A squad of soldiers walked past him and made him frown. Usually they patrolled in groups of two or three. He kept going, descending the stairs to the courtyard and looking around.

While he didn't see the tailor, he did notice a knight issuing orders to a group of soldiers.

"Sir Hayden," he called as he approached the man.

"Evander," the knight greeted.

"What's going on?" he asked curiously.

"Nothing to be concerned about. The princess was detained a town over. Her carriage broke an axle."

Evander frowned. *An axle?* "Oh. Then the guard?" A wheel he could understand, it was fairly common and an easy fix. The axle on the other hand was very difficult to break unless something went very, *very* wrong.

"Just extra precautions. Something doesn't sit well; Sir Michael has all of us on alert."

Evander hummed in agreement, so Sir Michael had had the same thought. "Have you heard anything from the royal tailor?"

"The tailor? He hasn't come in yet. Then again, I've been issuing orders, so I may have missed him. Ask the gate guards. They would have received a message if he were coming through."

"Thanks." Evander trotted off in the direction of the gate, the last line of defense before the castle itself.

There were three gates total that surrounded the castle. Each held a courtyard — a killing yard more specifically. Three walls, three gates, three large open spaces surrounded by murder holes and other mechanations that would wreak havoc on an attacking force before they ever neared the castle proper. Evander looked up at the wall that separated the castle from the noble's quarter, which took up the space between the third and fourth walls.

The design had been mimicked for the second quarter, leaving a courtyard to be used as a killing ground and gates protecting the wealthier-than-most commoners. Most of the buildings were for merchants, high class stores, restaurants, and the like. Most days, all of the gates remained open until nightfall. Today was no different, despite the increased guards and delayed princess.

The guards there saluted as he approached.

"Any sign of the tailor?" he asked.

"Tailor? That weaselly little guy that was here a couple of weeks ago?"

"That would be the one." He couldn't exactly admonish these two for voicing what he himself thought, even if it was rude.

"Haven't seen him. He hasn't checked in at the First Gate either."

Evander frowned. "Odd. Have a courier retrieve me when he arrives."

"Will do, Sir."

Evander turned on his heel and marched back to Caiden's room, knocking briefly before entering.

Caiden was sitting in the window seat, one of the small pamphlets on public speaking dangling from his fingers as he stared down at the gardens. He looked up as the servant entered.

"That was fast."

"Yes. The tailor is late, and the princess has been delayed."

The man immediately brightened, "So, I have the day off?"

"His Majesty invited you to lunch should your schedule allow it. Afterwards, you still have your lessons with Luten."

Caiden slouched and sighed, staring out the window again. "Could you fetch me my textbooks then?"

Evander gave him a blank stare. "Your textbooks?"

"They should be in the study."

His expression turned to narrow-eyed suspicion. "Of course, Your Highness." He gave the man a slight bow and turned to go and find the books.

When he returned, he found the guards shifting anxiously, biting their lips with mirth in their eyes. He sighed heavily as he opened the door, finding the prince gone. Again. He shot the guards a glare that made them both stand back to attention, then entered the room and closed the door.

Evander grumbled quietly to himself as he arranged the books on the table, pausing to pick up a few things that had fallen out of order in the prince's escape. He slowed to a stop, his hand still hovering over the pillow he'd just replaced on the window seat. A creeping feeling at his back that sent chills along his spine. His fingers trailed to one of his daggers as he turned around, finding the room to be empty.

He frowned and took a few steps forward, looking under the table and glancing around again. Nothing. He hummed, scanning over the room as he turned back to the window.

Only to come face to face with a girl. He jumped, swallowing the yell of surprise while a grin spread across her features.

"You'd be dead if I was after you, Eva."

Evander glared, recovering from his shock. He quickly cast a glance around the room, grabbing her arm and dragging her into his room, locking the doors and closing the window.

"The hell do you think you're doing, Riu?" he hissed.

She simply grinned and made herself comfortable on his bed. "What, no kiss hello?" She pouted playfully at him when he didn't move. "I can't stay in the Inner Castle all the time, you know. It gets dull after a while. Besides, something interesting is going on, don't you think?"

He watched as she played with a strand of her hair. "Do you know something?"

"I don't."

He stared at her and she stared back, her hazel eyes bright against her dark skin. If she didn't know, then it was something big and probably really, really bad. It made his stomach twist in excitement.

"Do you have any idea what Ansom will do if he finds you?"

"Skin me alive and hang my corpse out for all to see?" She shrugged. "Oh! Can I use your bath? I've been using Karen's sinks but it's a bit nerve wracking to be in the open so long." Even as she asked, she was discarding her clothing. Completely shameless. Not that he hadn't seen it all before.

He raised an eyebrow at her, not moving to get her water either.

"What? He's been looking for me for years now. I doubt he'll find me."

He shook his head and sat down in the chair by his desk. "So, what are you here for? You rarely ever make appearances and I seriously doubt it's just to make use of the bath."

Riu had been in the same tier as him in their group, one of the select few that were chosen as candidates for the royal Guardians. But, like him, her ability had been deemed useless and she had lost everything. Soul Swap, they called her. She could switch the souls of two people so they would occupy each other's bodies.

Unfortunately, it usually killed them and she couldn't use it on herself.

To top it off, she and Ansom fought badly a few years prior and she disappeared. She became known as the Watcher to those who knew about her. Always around, almost all-knowing, hiding in passageways that even the clan had long forgotten about.

It was rumored, briefly, that she was a spy. She was different, after all. She was of Coralian descent, a warm island nation that gave her her dark waving hair and deeply tanned skin. Her parents, or at least one of them, was Kepparin, which gave her her name. How she came to be in Kallenport was a mystery. However, Evander had known her since childhood, which meant she was young when the clan picked her up. Too young to have been sent as a spy. Besides, if she was against them, Kallenport would already be handed over to her superiors.

He'd be the first to admit she was far more clever than he was.

"Evander, what do you think will happen if Ansom takes over?" she asked, interrupting his musings as she came to stand in front of him, leaning over him and waiting. She was purposefully trying to be alluring but Evander ignored her advance with what had to be insulting ease.

He tilted his head back to look at her, easily adjusting his seat so she could comfortably brace her forearms against his shoulders to look down at him. Well, perhaps he wasn't completely immune. "I kill Caiden and be done with the whole ordeal. He'd have to do it before the coronation though. Considering that it's only a month away, I doubt he'd do such a thing."

"Really?" This time it was her turn to raise that questioning brow at him.

He tilted his head to the side and thought about it. "It would be pointless. Besides, Marie is more than capable."

"But if he did. What do you think would happen to you?"

"It's not like he can actually afford to kill me."

She shrugged. "I was just asking, Eva." She smirked at his loathed nickname.

He glared at her, "I'm not getting you water for your bath."

She threw her head back and laughed, a deep and brash sound that made something pleasant flutter through him. "Please?" she asked sweetly.

He held out for about five seconds before grumbling, "Fine."

# Chapter Three
Month of the Griffin 12, 421 HE

Evander jolted out of his sleep, woken by the thunderous call of the alarm bells. The deep booming sound echoed throughout the castle and would be heard and taken up by every town until the whole kingdom knew. The king was dead.

The king is dead. Attack on the castle.

Evander jumped out of bed, quickly putting on his gear. He could hear it now that he was fully awake. The singular bell that tolled several notes higher, its sound nearly drowned out by the alarm.

1...2...3... That was all Evander needed to hear. In order it went: the King, Queen, then the first born to be killed. It was their orders. Finally. He tightened his belt, his swords resting comfortably at his hip as he crossed to the door separating his room from Caiden's.

This was it. The order had been given. All it would take was one moment, one single moment. Evander pushed open the door.

And found the room empty.

He cursed and ran to Caiden's door, throwing it open and finding the guards that usually stood there to be absent. The halls were strangely quiet, the bells echoing through the empty space. There should have been chaos as everyone scrambled to get the ambassadors and nobles out of the castle, yet there was no such thing.

He frowned and started a brisk pace down the hall, following the sound of voices once he heard them. What he found in the nobles' wing of the castle made him pause. There were a large number of guards and knights, standing around a larger group of people ranging from nobles and ambassadors to servants. They seemed to be separating into three distinct groups and Evander shoved his way through until he could see Caiden in the middle of it all. Odder still was that rather than one of the knights directing the people, the prince himself seemed to be taking charge.

"Group One! Sir Michael will lead you out through this passage here. Group two, follow Sir Hayden. Group three will go with Sir Payne." The prince's voice carried easily through the crowd with a solid assuredness that kept everyone calm. Then he spotted Evander.

There was a strange look on the man's face as he made his way over to him.

"Eva, I need you to go with Sir Payne. He is the only one that I couldn't explain the passages to. You know the castle better than anyone."

It took him a moment to recover from his shock. "But—Your Highness—" *Dammit, there are too many witnesses.*

"That's an order, Evander." His tone stopped Evander dead in his tracks. *Impossible. Is this what he was always sneaking out for? He couldn't have possibly managed to acquire this much... charisma.*

Leadership skills: Check.

He glanced over the groups as one of the soldiers pulled Caiden aside to ask him something. They had been separated evenly so that even if one group was killed, people of the same strategic value may still survive.

Tactical ability: Check.

"Sir Payne!" Caiden called the knight over, "Evander will show you the way through the library passage."

"Yes, Sir." The knight saluted, his iron gauntlet making a satisfying clink as it hit the metal of his chest piece. Caiden turned away from them, starting down the hall.

"Your Highness! Where are you going?" Evander shouted after him as everyone started to move.

"Gathering any stragglers!" Caiden called over his shoulder as he started to run.

*Dammit.* He couldn't just run after him without—

"Get going."

Evander looked up at Sir Payne. "I can't just—"

"I can take care of this; the prince is your priority. Go."

"The brazier on the northern wall, between the stained-glass windows, will open the passage." Evander saluted the man who returned the gesture before the servant took off running.

*Where did he go?* He glanced through the side passages, searching for any sign of the prince's trail. *Ansom really will have my head if I let him get away.*

It was as he crossed one of the main halls that he came to the sudden realization; he was going to get Marie.

He put on a burst of speed, pacing himself so he would have more than enough energy to fight once it came to that. Kaitlyn should have evacuated the princess by now. Once Caiden paused to look for her, it would be the perfect opportunity to kill him.

He stumbled to a stop as he turned the corner, watching Caiden clean the blade of his sword on the back of a dead assassin. Miles. Not the most powerful of their order, but he hadn't been weak by any means.

*Where did he learn to fight?* He swore he'd been silent, but the prince seemed to sense him, whipping around and raising his sword in a defensive stance. He'd never seen the man lift a sword let alone fight anyone outside of their mandatory training, yet the ease with which he handled himself spoke of consistent practice.

"Eva? What are you doing here?" He straightened but to Evander's surprise, he didn't lower his sword. His surprise turned to shock as he trotted forward, and Caiden danced back.

Combat ability: Check.

"I came to find you." He stopped moving and raised his hands in a reassuring gesture.

"I told you to go with Sir Payne!"

"I'm not going to leave you here." *Not alive, at least.*

Caiden rolled his eyes, chewing on his lower lip as his eyes glanced about. "Fine. You lead. We need to find Marie."

Evander mentally tisked. Kind of hard to stab someone in the back when you were walking in front of them. He let it go. After all, once they got to the room and Caiden was looking for his sister, it would be easy to kill him.

Evander started down the hallway, easily navigating the eastern wing of the castle to get to the princess' rooms. They were situated at the end of the eastern wing, a dead end if you didn't know how to get into the servant's passages or into the Inner Castle. He looked up at the large window that framed the full moon as he turned down the princess's hall. They stopped in front of her door and at Caiden's gesture, he knocked.

Silence.

"She might be hiding. Just go in." Caiden's voice was hushed in the eerily quiet hall, the chaos far removed from their current location. Evander took a deep breath. He just had to get Caiden into the room.

"Marie? It's Eva. I'm coming in, okay?" he called, though he was sure she wouldn't be there. He shouldered open the door, taking two steps into the room before freezing.

Marie. Sweet, tiny, beautiful little Marie. Her body was sprawled out, still in her nightgown, a stuffed toy laying close to her hand. He recognized the tattered thing. It was something that he and Caiden had made for her when she'd fallen ill years prior. Her neck was twisted cruelly at an impossible angle, her strawberry blond curls laying bright across the rug. He didn't want to look, but he didn't have to. He could hear it now in his frozen state.

The high bell that tolled above the alarm. *1...2...3...* and there, *4*. She didn't need to die. She was perfect. She was the one. She was the perfect ruler. She wasn't supposed to die. Yet the evidence was there. Her death had been ordered.

"Eva?"

Evander jolted into motion again, backing up until he hit the prince's chest and he pushed, trying to keep Caiden from seeing past him. "Caiden, don't."

"Evander, move." Strong hands grabbed him by the shoulders and forcibly moved him aside. Evander watched the prince stand in his sister's doorway, processing what he was seeing. Then he watched him take a deep breath and straighten his spine. "Come on."

"What?"

"We have to go."

"But—"

"We need to make sure that everyone loyal to me gets out safely." The man's voice was strong as he pushed past him again.

Control over emotion: Check.

Kingdom first: Check.

The useless idiot suddenly wasn't so useless after all. Caiden met every requirement that they had in place. He was fit to rule. So why were they doing this? Why did

Marie have to die too? *Why?* The question repeated itself over and over in his head. Why were they doing this? *"He'd have to do it before the coronation."* Evander felt his stomach flip. Ansom was taking over the throne.

"Eva? Come on. We have to go." Caiden was looking back at him. Both of them turned towards the noise that was quickly approaching. There was a large group of people coming towards them, and Evander was willing to bet they weren't friendly. Caiden turned back to him, his eyes flicking back and forth, his hand tightening on his sword. He was trying to think of a plan.

Evander made his choice. And he broke into a dead sprint straight for the prince.

He ignored the blatant fear and surprise on the man's face at his fast approach, his arms rising into a defensive stance. Evander grabbed his arm on his way by. They couldn't use the passages. They'd be cornered. They reached the end of the princess's hall, where it met with the larger corridor. There was yelling and a glance showed Ansom and his group of elites coming towards them. He ran the other way, straight for the dead end. Straight for that bright, full moon, subtly activating his ability.

"EVANDER!" the infuriated roar echoed off the walls as Ansom's bloodlust and rage was made horrifyingly apparent. Evader didn't dare to look back, his hand tightening on the prince's arm and pulling him closer as he drew one of his heavier throwing daggers. He threw. Not at their pursuers but at the window, the heavy weapon cracking the glass.

"Eva!" Caiden screamed, catching on to what he was planning.

He realized too late that it had been a warning as a knife buried itself in his shoulder. He grit his teeth and jumped, twisting around Caiden as his uninjured shoulder hit the weakened glass and shattered it. Then they were falling.

Caiden clung onto him as he twisted, reaching for the castle wall. The moon threw their shadows against the stone and he tightened his hold on the prince as he activated his ability. The air felt squeezed from his lungs as he dragged them through the shadow itself, focused on the shrubbery below them. A moment of vertigo, and then he was dragging them onto solid ground at the base of the wall.

His head spun from the turnaround, but he had become used to the nauseating effect. Caiden, on the other hand, immediately started retching. He pulled the prince up and found his next target, on the other side of the courtyard just beside the gate. He grabbed Caiden and stepped into the nearest shadow, stepping out beside the portcullis.

The walls and all their tricks and traps, useless against an enemy from within. Now the killing yards could be used against anyone attempting to get in to help or those who were trying to flee.

Caiden was braced on his hands and knees beside him, dry heaving and dizzy if his swaying was anything to go by. Evander looked out past the iron gate and found the shadow of a building a short way down the road. He pulled the prince back to his feet and jumped into the shadow they'd just vacated.

His momentum carried them through to his destination, sending them airborne at an angle so he could hit the next shadow as he landed. The result was something that felt like a sickening form of flying and falling. It was going to hurt when he finally stopped, but it was something he was willing to take. So long as he maintained his focus, he would be able to keep going for hours.

But that wasn't taking into consideration his carrying the prince.

Caiden hadn't said anything, clinging desperately to him, and Evander could tell he was trying not to be sick again. He managed to keep them going for almost thirty minutes, increasing the distance between every shadow until he could feel his control straining with the speed that they were traveling at. They had gone miles. He had no idea where they were or what direction they were going in. He only knew that he had to keep moving.

Caiden suddenly became a deadweight. The sudden pull tore into his shoulder, making him yelp, remembering the knife that was still stuck deep in the tissue. His focus snapped. He barely had time to try and slow them down, thickening the shadow they were about to jump through, dragging them through it rather than falling into it. It deposited them almost thirty yards away from their prior location.

He landed on his hands and knees, his limbs trembling with fatigue. His head ached and he coughed, bile rising in the back of his throat. They couldn't stop.

They had to keep going. He clenched his hands into fists and hissed as even that small action brought searing pain to his shoulder. He spat and dragged himself up to his feet, pulling at Caiden.

The prince groaned, and Evander knew that his body would feel battered and bruised.

"Get up!"

Caiden gave a soft moan and rolled over, trying to get up to his hands and knees. He fell back to the ground after swaying for a moment.

"Get up!" Evander yanked the man to his feet and Caiden blinked deliriously at him. Evander shook him, only able to use one arm for the task. "Do you hear me? Get. Up. Now."

Caiden squinted at him, his head rolling back and forth.

"Focus on me. Got it? You have to move."

Caiden squeezed his eyes shut, and Evander could see his attempt to breathe and control how his head was spinning. Then the prince opened his eyes again and Evander was relieved to see that they were clear. Then those eyes widened, trailing to his side.

Evander winced, knowing he shouldn't look. As soon as the adrenaline wore off, he was screwed. That's why he needed the prince to move.

He followed Caiden's gaze and saw his right side soaked through with blood. He must have moved too much. The blade was still in him, keeping the wound from bleeding as profusely but looking at it now... well... maybe the spinning in his head wasn't completely from using his ability. And maybe the shaking wasn't just from fatigue... now that he thought about it... he really was not feeling well...

"Eva?" He could feel Caiden's hands trying to steady him, trying to keep him upright. "Hey, wait!"

"Heh... shit. Really should have seen this coming..." Evander blearily looked around, finding them deep in the forest, surrounded by hills as the sun began to rise. Not a single sign of civilization. He sighed in relief and finally caved to the painless bliss that was teasing the edges of his mind.

# Chapter Four
Month of the Griffin 14, 421 HE

He felt as though his mind was swimming through murky water. He felt cold, chilled, and his skin, felt clammy as though he'd been sweating. There was a dull pain that pulsed through his body with every beat of his heart.

Evander slowly forced his eyes open, finding himself face down on some sort of cot. The room was dusty and dark, the air stale as though it had been abandoned or at least had been empty for some time. He was looking at a chipped basin that sat on a table, a cloth slung over the edge.

He shivered, the movement making him realize that the knife was gone and his right arm was numb. Pain shot up his neck and he groaned, attempting to move again only for the pain to double. He laid down in defeat as the soft sound of footsteps approached him. He couldn't even bring himself to look.

He heard the gentle sound of water sloshing in the basin, being wrung out before the cloth touched his skin.

He winced as something was peeled off of his shoulder and someone hummed in thought. He finally opened his eyes again, looking up at Caiden as the man examined his wounds. The Prince didn't look at him, as though he didn't expect him to be awake. He looked exhausted, dark circles standing out in the candlelight, a tightness in the corner of his mouth and in his shoulders.

Caiden turned away from him for a moment, leaving his line of sight before returning with a small bowl in his hand.

"What're you doing?" Evander's voice was rough, his throat parched.

Caiden looked down at him, surprise painted on his pale face. He didn't reply, setting aside the bowl and lifting the cloth again. Evander sighed as the cool water was passed over his neck and the side of his face before Caiden laid the cloth over his eyes.

"Go back to sleep. When you wake, all will be well again." Those familiar words resounded in him like a magic spell and he found himself relaxing as skilled fingers pressed into the base of his skull. The sting in his shoulder was drowned out by the relief in his pounding head as something was pressed to the wound.

He remembered vaguely why the actions felt familiar, why those words put him at ease. The court Physician, Jedidiah, had said those same words to him years prior. He'd fallen ill. No one had known what had caused it, but children all throughout the city had fallen ill with fever. Marie had been sick with it as well. She had survived, and everyone had thought that the sickness had passed. Caiden never caught it and Evander had been fine until he collapsed nearly a month after the last case had been cured.

He'd been kept isolated. The only contact he'd had was with the Physician. He'd never really spoken to the man before that, or even afterwards. Besides thanking him, Evander never had the need to visit. After all, most of his injuries were caused by the Clan and were healed by Karen.

Even the way Caiden went about treating him struck him as familiar from those days that he'd spent in Jedidiah's care.

--†--
## Griffin, 19

He didn't remember falling asleep, but he woke to rough, tuneless humming and sunlight. The shutters were open, letting in the late summer breeze. He could see what looked like a clothesline outside.

He slowly sat up, finding that he had limited control of his arm now, which was much better than the numbness that had been there when he'd last woken. His head didn't feel like it was going to split and while he felt sore and weak, he was no longer helpless.

Or at least that's what he'd thought. His head spun as soon as he tried to stand. He cursed and sat back down, holding his head and staring at a knot in the wooden floorboards to try and control it.

"You won't be able to move for a while." Caiden's voice made him look up at the man as he came inside, a basket of clean linens in his arms.

Evander looked around, discovering the place to be a tiny hunting cabin. It was clean and airy with the windows open. The small stove that sat over the fireplace held a steaming kettle, and it looked like potatoes were roasting in the embers. A basket of vegetables and fruit sat to the side and to Evander's surprise, a string of hares was hung there as well.

He held still as Caiden approached him, peeling something off of his shoulder again. This time, Evander watched closely as the man brought some sort of green glop-covered bandage away. His stomach twisted at the yellow tint, the reek of puss, and some type of sour odor.

"Poison?" he questioned.

"Snake venom," Caiden provided, throwing the bandage into a bucket beside the bed. "You shouldn't have moved like that while the knife was in you. It circulated a lot faster. You're lucky I didn't have to remove your arm."

Evander paled at the thought. "Where did you learn all of this?"

"Jedidiah. Where do you think I went to hide from you?" Caiden chuckled. He was rifling through the clean linens, pulling out a long bandage that looked suspiciously like a shredded sheet. He came back to him and Evander sat still as the man wrapped his shoulder and put his right arm into a sling.

It was true, Evander rarely ever went to the physician's quarters for anything and really, he didn't mind the impromptu free time. He never actually looked very hard for Caiden when the prince disappeared. After all, if Evander didn't have eyes on Caiden, Riu did. If either of them didn't, then at least one of them knew exactly where he was and what he was doing and had confidence in the people around him. So, yes, the physician's quarters were the perfect hiding spot.

"Here." Caiden held out his hand and Evander looked up at him with open suspicion. "You need to go outside for a while. Fresh air and sunshine can do wonders, you know."

"How long have we been here?" he asked, slowly allowing Caiden to help him up. He resisted the urge to pull away when the prince slung his good arm over his shoulders and wrapped an arm around his waist, supporting the majority of his weight as he led him outside. The strength that the man held surprised him. He had never known Caiden to enjoy sports or swordplay, nothing that would give him this amount of muscle.

He winced at the late summer sun as Caiden gently lowered him into a rocking chair that was sitting in front of the cabin. He felt... fragile. It was highly unpleasant. Then Caiden pulled up a stool and sat. "Roughly a week," the prince finally answered him.

"A week?" Evander frowned. "There's no way I could have just slept through a week."

"No, not naturally." Caiden's gaze slid to the side. "I had to wake you a few times to get you to eat and drink."

*So he kept me drugged to keep me asleep.*
Evander bit back his immediate response to the 'not
naturally' bit of Caiden's statement. He would have done
the same had their roles been reversed.

They sat in silence for a few moments until
Evander sighed and leaned back, basking in the warmth.
His mind was coming around in slow degrees. He was
processing the clean pants he wore that were unfamiliar
to him, the freshly made garden that had clearly just been
planted, the bow and quiver by the door, and the
complete lack of weaponry that was available to him.
Even his armor was gone."So…" Evander cleared his
throat, looking back at the prince who looked just as lost
as he was.

"Explain." The demand was quiet, and almost
fragile.

Evander sighed. "Where would you like me to
start?"

Caiden glared. "Oh, I don't know, how about we
start with why the hell my family is dead." his voice rose
and snapped, making Evander flinch.

He floundered for the words he needed. "This…
this wasn't supposed to happen." *Great start.* Evander
rubbed his temple with his uninjured hand. *This isn't
going to go well.*

"That doesn't explain anything."

"It's hard to explain."

"Try me."

Evander openly glared at the man.

"Eva… I already know." Caiden's voice was soft,
his face a sorrowful mask of self-loathing.

*Know what?* He wondered. *Which of the hundreds of secrets do you already know?* "Then why do I need to explain anything?"

"Because I want to know why it happened."

Evander sighed again. *Okay, state the obvious first.* "Ansom... Ansom took the throne. The clan, all of us, we are assassins. Our best were assigned to each member of the royal household to watch and guard them, to judge them and make sure that the kingdom would prosper under their rule."

Caiden frowned and tilted his head. "But..."

"You fit every tenet we had. Even if you didn't, Marie..." Evander's heart twisted painfully, the final image of her body burned into his mind. "She shouldn't have been killed if that were the case."

"That's why Princess Eudora was delayed," Caiden mused.

"Most likely." He observed the tired prince. It was strange to talk with him like this. "Ansom had to usurp the throne before your coronation. He was running out of time."

"Why?"

"Because once you took the throne, I would technically become the head of the clan." He smiled bitterly at the blank look of shock that Caiden gave him. "If it ever came to that, then I would be the one on the throne since I was your closest confidant."

Caiden was silent for a few moments. "But they want you dead. Why would they repeatedly try to harm you if you are the next in line?"

Evander froze. Stared. "What do you mean by that?" he asked slowly, observing every motion and expression that the prince made.

Caiden looked him dead in the eye and didn't even flinch. "I already told you, didn't I? I *know*."

Evander stared at him for what felt like a long while, his mind flying through the prior years, wondering how. How had Caiden found out? When? Then the thought occurred to him, what all had he seen? *He can't possibly know about... about* everything. *He'd have done something about it.* Caiden was not tolerant of certain things. Harm coming to Evander was one.

Caiden seemed to read the questions running through his head. "It was after… it was when Brian was killed."

Evander frowned at the mention of the stable master that had been executed for having magic.

"I sneaked into your room that night. I couldn't sleep at all. I was so nervous thinking about how mad you'd be…" The prince chuckled. "I just didn't want to be alone. But you weren't there. I thought maybe you were still running errands and I decided to wait." Caiden's eyes were unfocused, gazing at a scene long past. "The wardrobe doors were open, and I thought maybe you were hiding. So, I decided to look in. I saw that there was a passage and I followed it without thinking."

Evander remembered that night. It had been shortly after his ability had manifested. Ansom had wanted to beat it into his head that it could be him next. Could be any of them if anyone ever found out that they had magic. It had been the first time that he'd been beaten so badly. He had tried to use his ability while sparring with Ansom himself. It had infuriated the man.

Then again, Evander had been so young and there had been so many incidents after that that he didn't actually remember why Ansom had been so angry.

"I left when you were done, listened for when you'd gone to bed again before going in. After that, I used to watch almost every night."

Evander sighed, running a hand over his face. "So, if you knew, then why didn't you say anything?" He wondered for a moment if perhaps that was why Caiden came to sleep with him. He'd always found it unnerving how the prince only ever came after he'd gone to bed, despite his odd hours. Thinking of it now, those nights corresponded with disturbing accuracy with days that Evander had reason to be particularly hurt, or threatened.

"Because they would have killed you. It's normal for our personal bodyguards to have secret training rooms and special talents. I didn't think anything of it for a long time. It wasn't until recently that I thought there might be something wrong."

The fear, the paranoia that Caiden had shown towards him that night. It made sense now. He hadn't thought about it, hadn't had the chance. The lack of surprise at his ability was also explained. Caiden *knew*. It was strange trying to retroactively piece together the prince's capabilities, his intelligence. Evander found himself irritated to realize just how off-base his assumptions had been about the man that he'd known for most of his life.

Caiden might as well have been a stranger.

That thought in particular made Evander feel slightly nauseated. Or perhaps that was the aftereffects of the venom.

"Why didn't you just let me die?" he asked, the weight of the situation settling in.

"Why didn't you just kill me?" Caiden countered with a bitter smirk.

They lapsed back into silence, neither wanting to give their reason if they had one. Evander, for his part, didn't know the answer. He'd thought he hated Caiden, wanted him dead. Ansom was cruel, but he was intelligent and dutiful. Evander hadn't thought anything of letting Ansom rule years ago in place of the King. He hadn't even minded had it been now with the intention of giving the crown to Marie.

Marie. Sweet, little Marie. He'd never get to see her smile again. Never see her blush, hear her giggle. He'd never again be subjected to her running leaps into his arms, acting for all the world like a spoiled little girl who only knew love and happiness.

That had been what made his decision. Seeing her murdered in cold blood for no good reason just so that bastard could have and keep the throne? Evander would kill him for it. He swore it. How the hell did the madman expect to get away with it?

*Did he buy off the council?* Evander pondered over that thought and the implications of it for a few long moments. "So, what now?" he finally asked, watching as the Prince looked up at him. "You know everything. I'll tell you whatever you want. Doesn't really matter now."

"Well, I'm sure not everyone was killed. There has to be people still loyal to me out there, I'm sure they'll be looking for me."

"So will Ansom."

"What is Ansom's ability?" Caiden asked suddenly.

"Impeccable Aim. That's what we call it. If he throws anything with the intent to hit... well, it hits."

"Your abilities have names?"

Evander nodded.

"What's Karen's called?"

Evander could feel how his brows raise in surprise, but he supposed that if Caiden had been watching then it was only natural that he knew who the others were. "From the Brink."

"Huh. Fitting."

Evander frowned, and Caiden chuckled.

"I kind of had firsthand experience with that one."

Evander didn't have the chance to question him further before Caiden asked another question.

"So, if Ansom always has perfect aim, how did he miss you? I'm pretty sure he was aiming to kill when he threw that knife."

Evander shrugged. "It's possible that he wanted to watch me writhe in agony beforehand." It wasn't something that he'd put beyond the bastard.

Caiden gave him a disbelieving look. "I'm pretty sure he knows you well enough to know that you'll keep going unless you're dead."

Evander blinked at the unintentional compliment. "I never really tried it before, but it is possible that I skewed his ability."

"How so?"

Evander let a small smile show as he activated his ability, feeling for the shadows beneath the chair that he sat in. The darkness cast by his own body, the tiny dips and discrepancies in his skin. Then he pulled. The shadows shifted and threaded together, making his form waver. He laid it over himself, the second mass positioned an inch to the right.

Caiden stared at him for a moment until Evander released it. "Well, here I thought I was seeing things. So Ansom aimed at the wrong place. The heart on your shadow was your shoulder on... well, you."

"I wasn't exactly thinking about it at the time. I just knew he was going to try and kill me. You helped though. I was able to hide most of my actual body behind you, so he couldn't tell what I'd done from so far away."

"And what if he aimed for me?"

Evander smiled tiredly at him. "I think you underestimate his hatred for me. Besides, without my ability your escape was hopeless."

Caiden hummed in thought for a moment. "So, what is your ability called?"

This time Evander grinned, propping his cheek on his fist as he replied, "Shadow Dancer."

# Chapter Five
Month of the Griffin 29, 421 HE

"Eva, you really need to sit." Caiden's voice was not placating but more the tone of a bored parent repeating a warning for the thousandth time to an unruly child.

"Make me," Evander growled, only supporting the child's role that he found himself in.

Caiden sighed. "The worst part of that statement is that it would take me absolute minimal effort to accomplish that."

"You wouldn't."

"Sit. Down."

Evander glared at the man and finally slunk over to the rocking chair that he'd claimed since the day he'd woken up. "Jackass."

"That's no way to talk to a prince, you know."

"King," Evander idly corrected while Caiden skinned a rabbit. He watched the expert glide of the knife, keeping the skin perfectly intact as he revealed the meat.

It was something he'd watched Karen do hundreds of times.

"Heh. I really don't want to think of that right now." Caiden started humming again, tone-deaf as per usual. It wasn't unpleasant so long as he didn't try to actually sing. There was something charming about the off-handed tune.

It had been roughly ten days since he'd woken up and they had fallen into a semblance of a routine. Evander found himself at a loss for the most part. He was going stir crazy, unable to do much more than shuffle to and from the chair and bed. If he did anything more, the fever would come back.

Caiden claimed that he was almost cured, though he still insisted on force-feeding him some kind of Gods-awful concoction of crushed herbs every morning. His strength was returning in slow degrees, his control over his arm getting better with each passing day. But he was bored. Bedrest did not agree with him. At all.

It was odd. Caiden was attentive and careful, helping him through everyday tasks as though he had done such things his whole life. Evander had made a comment and Caiden had just grinned at him.

*"Think of it as my repaying you for fourteen years of taking care of me."*

Evander had grumbled. Honestly, he wasn't entirely comfortable being the one taken care of. He'd always taken care of Caiden. What he hated even more was that Caiden was good at it. They'd bickered a few times. Caiden was almost too good at all of these menial tasks. Evander had found him by the river early on, on a sunny day when he'd dared to walk farther than the immediate clearing.

*The prince had a large bucket and a handmade wooden mold. Evander kept quiet, watching as Caiden pried the lid off of the bucket, a cloth tied around his face to protect himself from whatever he was dealing with.*

*Evander caught a whiff of something distinctly unpleasant and it took him a moment to place it as lye, a strong chemical used in soap making. It was extremely dangerous and poisonous even to breath too much of the fumes. He waited until Caiden was finished dealing with the chemical. Once sure he wouldn't startle the prince into burning himself with it, Evander immediately demanded an explanation.*

*Caiden was surprised. "You're scared of my dealing with lye? It's not like I'm drinking it. Even if I did, don't you know antidotes?"*

*Evander stared at him incredulously "Poisons aren't my specialty. I know how to recognize them and I know how to use them. I don't know how to mix or cure them!"*

*"Oh? Here I thought you were good at everything." Caiden clearly wasn't listening to him.*

*"What the hell gave you that idea?" Evander growled, annoyed. "I know how to run a kingdom. I know how to fight. That's the extent of my job. I'm basically an elite butler and bodyguard. You, on the other hand, should know how to be a king and yet you're... what, making soap?"*

*Caiden stared at him blankly. "I... yes. Soap. We need to get everything done before winter so we don't have to go outside unless necessary. We need soap because we don't have the supplies to support either of us getting sick, so I've been busy trying to get the proportions right."*

*"You don't even know if you're doing it correctly?" Evander didn't know if he should be annoyed or shocked. "How did you even learn how to do any of this?"*

*"Remember how I told you I would help Jed?"*

*"Yes."*

*"I also used to help Karen. She would occasionally get sick of me being in her way and claim I was her nephew, sending me off with some servant or another. They were always one of the Vladimir clan and they were good enough at playing along to teach me various things." Caiden shrugged. "Honestly, Eva, for as much time as we spent together, we spent a lot of time apart for a pair who are supposed to be glued at the hip," he grinned.*

*Evander blinked. It was true. "I... spent that time training." He crouched beside the prince. Clearly, it was unexpected, and Caiden was silent, waiting for Evander to continue. "I was never very good at fighting, originally that is. I was clumsy and I didn't enjoy hurting people, so I was always hesitant." He turned and looked at Caiden, who didn't seem surprised.*

*"I've seen you practice," Caiden confided. "You were obsessive there for a while."*

*Evander chuckled. "I didn't think it was fair, the way I was shoved aside by Ansom. I thought if I was perfect in every other way, then my ability wouldn't matter. So, I practiced. A lot." He felt his face flush in embarrassment. "I'm still not that great at anything not involving combat or government. I'm good at directing people, but I can't do a whole lot by myself."*

*Caiden smiled and they'd sat in companionable silence for a while until the prince remembered that Evander should be in the cabin resting.*

Evander sighed and glared at the door. The wind was howling outside with a late summer storm, probably one of the last before the cooler weather started to set in. It was concerning. If Caiden was keeping track of the days since they'd escaped the Castle, then it meant that it was roughly the twenty-ninth in the month of the Griffin. It was the very end of summer, quickly giving way to autumn. They were running out of time.

Caiden was doing well, hunting and skinning so they would have warm furs and preserving fruits and meats that would keep through the winter. However, they were lacking in supplies to keep much more than a single month's worth of food.

They'd found a few heavy quilts in a trunk beneath the bed, but with the two of them it would be a bit of a struggle to keep warm. Especially since neither of them had any other clothes. They could only make so much with the furs that Caiden was attempting to tan.

They needed to get out of the kingdom. They needed to find a town or a farm. They needed salt, clothes, sewing supplies, winter boots, but Evander's main concern was with what to do when the owner of the cabin came. It looked like a winter hunting cabin, abandoned in the spring and summer but stocked with thick blankets and built to retain heat? Definitely used in the colder months.

"Quit worrying about it," Caiden's voice rang through his thoughts.

He blinked at him, finding the prince easily cutting apart the hare. "I wasn't worrying."

"You're always worrying."

Evander glared but when it became apparent that Caiden wasn't going to continue that line of conversation, he sighed. Casting a wary glance at the prince, he slowly stretched his arms out in front of him. There was a slight pull in his shoulder where the wound was still tender, but otherwise his arm was recovering fine. He didn't need to wear a sling anymore at least.

He relaxed, staring at the small fire that was dancing in the hearth. A fox was roasting on a spit, some water boiling on the side. Caiden was a much better cook than Evander liked to give him credit for. He also had a wide array of skills that Evander never knew of. Cooking, herbalism, healing, hunting, skinning, tanning, fletching, trapping, laundering...

He switched his focus to the world outside, the sudden quiet signaling the end of the storm. He pushed himself up out of the chair and wandered over to the window, unlatching the wooden shutters and pushing them open.

The sky was grey and dreary, rain drizzling at an ever-slowing pace. He breathed in deep, the scent of the fresh dirt and wet grass refreshing after being cooped up. He heard Caiden sigh behind him and his shoulders slumped, lounging half out the window in a rather undignified pout as he waited for the man to make good on his threat.

Rather than being physically put to bed, he was handed a basket. Evander stared at it, then looked at Caiden.

"If you aren't going to sit, then could you at least go gather some more herbs? We need more mint, yarrow, burdock, and lavender. They're a bit harder to identify now with the flowers dying, but there are a few in the bottom, there, that you can compare to. Just don't go past the stream, the fallen oak, or the meadow."

Evander raised an eyebrow at him. "What, are you my mother now?"

"I didn't think you had a mother, Eva," Caiden replied sweetly with a sarcastic smile.

Evander's raised eyebrow lowered into a narrow-eyed glare. "Right. Stay in the area, I get it." He snatched the basket from him and marched out the door.

It was chilly now with the sun hiding behind the remaining rain clouds. He sighed as he walked, following the lightly trodden path that Caiden usually used.

It had come up at some point over the last week, his origins. Truth be told, Evander didn't really know who his parents were, and he'd told Caiden that.

*"But, how did you get to the castle then?"*
*"I was raised there for as long as I can remember. Might've been born there, for all I know."*
*"How do you not know?"*
*"Well, most of the clan are either taken from their parents as babies or they're kind of... bred?"*
*Caiden stared at him, horrified. "You kidnap children?"*
*Evander shrugged. "Not really. They are given up. Left in temples or by roadsides. They would have died within the year if the clan didn't pick them up."*
*"But why would they—?"*
*"Caiden, every single one of us has magic. We would have been killed before reaching our second year if the mage-hunters passed through. So many were simply... murdered. Personally, I think it's better to pick them up and give them somewhere to live. Even if it is as assassins."*
*"So, what about you?"*
*"I'm pretty sure I was born to two of the clan members. Malik might have been my father, but I never knew my mother. Or at least, I have no memory of her."*
*"Malik? As in my grandfather's advisor?"*
*Evander nodded.*

He smiled slightly at the memories that came from that train of thought. The clan children were all raised communally so that there were no long-lasting attachments between members. After all, if any one of them were found out and executed, it would be a mess if their children accidentally outed themselves. Or a spouse.

However, he remembered a large hand patting his head and a kind, doting smile as he was lifted up and set in a warm lap. *"A parent is a parent. No amount of paranoia or forced tradition will ever change that."* He remembered that warm feeling that spread through his very soul at the notion that he was so undoubtedly loved by that man. He was only five when Malik left. The old predecessor, Caiden's grandfather, left for a small villa to live out the rest of his days and Malik had gone with him. It was the last time anyone ever saw or heard from him.

That was when Ansom took over the clan.

He shook himself out of his thoughts, looking around at the foliage. He frowned, examining the herbs in his basket and starting to wander through the trees, searching for anything similar.

An hour later, he was about ready to throw the basket at Caiden's head when he got back. He hadn't found a damn thing and had spent the last twenty minutes trying to figure out if the plant in his hand was lavender, or just a weed that looked like lavender. Or was he looking at yarrow?

He couldn't tell what was what. As he'd told Caiden, he knew how to recognize poisons. In fact, there was a nice patch of wolf's bane only a few feet away. He was completely lost as to what medical plants to look for. Even knowing that the plant in front of him was wolfsbane he had no clue what to do with it if he picked it.

He looked up at the sky, seeing that the sun was starting to decline. He slowly stood and dusted off his knees.

*Time to go back.* He had never gone this far from the cabin and while he was sure that he could at least find his way back, he didn't want to do so in the dark. He sighed and rolled his shoulders. Caiden had probably sent him out just to get some fresh air and exercise, knowing he wouldn't actually find anything. Bastard.

Evander gathered the random assortment of likely weeds and threw them in his basket starting to head back along the trail. An odd yet familiar tingle crawled down his spine and settled uncomfortably in his gut. Something wasn't right. There were no birds singing. It was quiet. Very, very quiet. He walked a little faster, straining his hearing, trying to catch anything out of place.

A twig snapped behind him, the distinctive crunch of a footfall on the dead leaves.

He bolted, flinging the basket aside in favor of using his arms to help gain momentum. Yells sounded behind him. Whoops and hollers as his pursuers abandoned their stealth. There were at least five of them.

Evander mentally cursed as he vaulted over a fallen tree. He couldn't lead them back to Caiden. They weren't Ansom's elites, nor were they soldiers.

*Bandits? Why the hell are there bandits?* There hadn't been a bandit problem for the last eight years. Damn vultures must've heard about the coup and thought they could get some loot from the chaos. Of course, it was his luck that he'd run into one of the only bands of ruffians in the kingdom, if they weren't swarming the whole area.

"Eva!"

He dove to the side without thinking, an arrow streaking past his head close enough to stir his hair. One of the men behind him must have been much faster than he'd thought because the roar of pain was far too close for comfort.

He skidded to a stop, spinning around as he reached Caiden's position to see a small handful of people fanning out around them.

"And to think, you were always worried about me getting into trouble." Caiden chuckled, tossing aside his bow and drawing two swords from his belt, handing one to Evander.

"I still worry about you getting into trouble. You should have stayed put."

There were four bandits now, with the fifth attempting to drag herself away with Caiden's arrow through her chest. Evander put a stop to that before the others could move. Now there were three men, one woman. They looked average, experienced with their weapons but far from professional. One of them was of a monstrous size, wielding an axe that Evander wanted to stay well clear of. They were outnumbered, but Evander didn't want them to find the cabin either. It didn't leave them with much of a choice but to fight.

The big one charged at them, likely trying to split them apart so they'd be easier to pick off. Had Caiden spent more time training in combat perhaps they would have been able to circumvent the maneuver, but as it was they ended up with the axe-wielder between them. They were still close enough to easily communicate and with a bit of effort, they may be able to get rid of the big one.

Evander quickly reevaluated their chances as the brute brought his axe down against his sword and his shoulder strained. He tilted the weapon away, trying to disengage. He could see Caiden over the bandit's shoulder. He was keeping his back close to the axe-wielder so the other bandits couldn't get behind him. It was impressive. The prince had a reaction speed on par with some of the Vladimir clan's members. Against three people, he was taking care to keep himself guarded. They didn't have enough room to rush him without getting in each other's way, but that would only last until the axe-wielder turned around.

So, it fell to Evander to keep the big guy busy.

The brute pushed forward, forcing Evander back a step as he deflected one blow, then back another as he dodged the next. The bandit grinned as he swung again and Evander jumped backwards, slamming into the trunk of a tree.

He cursed, barely getting his sword up in time to catch the blade of the axe, having to brace his sword with his uninjured hand as his sword arm buckled. There was no escape. It was almost a blessing that he was braced against the tree, else he didn't think he could hold up the sheer weight of the man behind the axe. He could try to redirect the blow, but it could, no, *would* kill him if he failed.

His arms were outright shaking now, his left hand bloody from where the blade was digging into his palm. He mentally swore, scrambling for some sort of plan, some kind of escape— he blinked. He could do that.

Caiden's back was to him, but Evander could see the frequent glances that the prince was throwing towards him. He couldn't help without leaving himself exposed to the other three bandits.

"Caiden!" Evander shouted.

"Yeah?" came the ground out reply as the prince blocked a blow and shoved the bandit back.

"Tag out."

Caiden spared him a quick glance, confused, and then Evander grinned as the understanding seemed to dawn on the man.

*Evander sighed, watching Caiden and one of the soldiers spar. The trainee was around the same age as the prince, if not a bit older, with Caiden being thirteen. Sir Michael stood next to him, arms crossed over his barrel chest.*

*"Begin!" The shout rang in Evander's ears, but his attention was on the pair in the middle of the training grounds.*

*He knew Caiden hated fighting. He wasn't the greatest at it and he refused to practice enough to get better. In a real fight, he'd be dead in half a heartbeat.*

*At least that's what he'd thought.*

*Caiden had a good instinct. He knew when to block and dodge but he didn't quite have the timing down to make a good hit. The trainee was a proud young greenhorn who clearly had it in his head that beating Caiden would make him look good.*

*After a few strikes, it was clear that the brat was holding back enough to keep the prince from losing but it was bordering on bullying. He was practically chasing Caiden around the circle, hitting hard enough to hurt but not hard enough for Sir Michael to call him out.*

*However, Caiden wasn't yielding. He was taking the beating and refusing to surrender.*

*Evander looked up at Sir Michael as the knight's hand landed heavily upon his shoulder.*

*"Tag out."*

*Evander gave a nod and inconspicuously picked up a pair of short swords, positioning himself just to the edge of the ring. At Sir Michael's nod, he sprinted forward.*

Evander focused on Caiden's shadow and reached for the shadow of the bandit he was fighting. He'd never tried to use his ability on a shadow that was already touching him, but he didn't have enough time to think about it as the brute drew back a fraction only to throw the entirety of his weight into the blow.

Rather than moving through a portal as he was used to, the shadow seemed to absorb him. He emerged from behind Caiden and the prince jumped away, whether the reaction was out of shock or if the man was trying to give him room to move, was up for debate. The axe-wielder gave a shout of alarm as he crashed face first into the tree that Evander had been braced against.

Caiden was quick about disposing of him, but Evander caught the brief hesitation before the Prince's blade sank into the bandit's side. That would have to be trained out of him.

The three others were trying to take advantage of Caiden's distraction, not realizing that Evander was there. He quickly changed that, stabbing through the first one that was too focused on Caiden to react in time. The remaining two skidded to a halt, seeing that half their force was dead and they were now evenly matched.

And the tables had turned in the span of a heartbeat. They were clearly still dumbfounded. Evander found himself grinning, and he knew the expression was practically maniacal judging by the bandits' hesitation. It was down to the female and the youngest of the males.

The young man charged at him with a yell and Evander easily locked blades with him. He winced, his arms still tired from holding up the brute for so long. It wasn't anything more than an inconvenience, but the woman was turning to run and Evander didn't think he could move fast enough to catch her.

"Get her!" he snapped at Caiden, shoving the bandit he was dealing with back enough to get his sword into a better position. Inexperience showed itself when the young man didn't back off and instead tried to come at him again. Evander sighed as his blade drove into the bandit's stomach at an upward angle, easily bypassing the thickest points of the meager armor and striking the heart. The angle meant it was harder to withdraw his blade in a hurry and as he glanced up, he saw Caiden still hesitating and the woman quickly getting farther away.

Evander grabbed a dagger off the young bandit's belt as he dropped the body and sword together, taking only two steps before throwing the weapon. It wasn't balanced properly so it struck lower than he intended.

It still did the job and the woman pitched forward, lying in an ominously still heap on the forest floor. Had she thought to weave through the trees, she wouldn't have been hit. Evander found he had very little pity for her.

He frowned and squinted, realizing that the clearing was far too dark to be natural, especially after only five— no, maybe only a minute of fighting. He could never tell how much time passed in combat. Belatedly, he realized that he'd been using his magic and released it. Sunlight poured through the trees, illuminating red-tinted mud and ruined grass.

"We make a pretty decent team, don't we?" The offhanded, cheerful tone sounded forced and brought his attention to Caiden who was cleaning his blade on the back of one of the bandits.

"What're you smiling about?" Evander asked irritably as he walked over and wrenched his sword free of his last kill. Being only a step away from Caiden, he could see the prince's hands, white knuckled around the hilt of his sword and trembling. Evander had a feeling it wasn't from fear. Perhaps from the adrenaline. He elected to wipe his sword clean with a cloth pulled from one of the corpses, thinking over the encounter.

"Nothing much. I think you might be cured though. Or at least well enough to handle moving around without courting death." The man wandered over to stand beside him as Evander stood.

*Ah. First kill.* He made the realization as he looked over at the prince. Caiden was staring almost blankly at the bandit by his feet. Even if his face held a smile, he wasn't mentally coping as well as someone who'd been trained to take lives from a young age.

Granted, it wasn't actually the prince's first. He'd killed Miles back at the castle. But that had been a time of confusion and fear and Caiden did what had to be done. The prince had defended himself against a lone assassin. An outnumbered battle where no one would come to your rescue even if you screamed was something a little different.

"Oh good, perfect timing." He grinned, and Caiden gave him a suspicious look. Suspicious, but no longer dull. "Because I wanted to try something."

He didn't give the prince any warning before he struck with his blade, catching the man by surprise as he spun the short sword in his hand, hitting him with the hilt instead of the edge. Caiden coughed as it smacked into his diaphragm, forcing him to double over.

"What the hell?" The words came out strangled.

Evander smirked at him. "I think it might be worth teaching you a thing or two."

# Chapter Six
Month of the Maiden 12, 421 HE

Evander hummed, circling Caiden in the clear area outside of the cabin. "You have a stable fighting stance, but it doesn't allow for much movement,"

The prince was watching him carefully, having learned from the numerous bruises that Evander was more of a 'learn by doing' type of teacher. Evander had to admit, it was extremely satisfying to be able to beat Caiden, even after being weakened by the poison.

They had been training for two weeks since the bandit attack, Evander honing Caiden's rusty skills into something that was almost proficient. Though, he had to admit, it was easier since the man was mimicking his own fighting style and adapting it to his strengths.

*"So, where did you learn to fight?" Evander asked slowly as they stripped the bandits of their possessions. While he hadn't gone on the offensive with the bandits, he had done very well defending. Something that Evander knew didn't come from his formal training.*

*Caiden looked over at him. "From you. I told you, Eva, I've always been watching. Granted, I made Sir Hayden practice with me every once in a while, when he wasn't busy."*

*Evander stared at him. Sir Hayden won his knighthood on the battlefield. He'd been the Battle Master's Second in Command for years.*

*"That's where you got that scar from, isn't it?" he asked.*

*Caiden grinned sheepishly. "Yeah, I told him not to go easy on me and he agreed. Karen healed me after a particularly vicious match," he grumbled, clearly remembering being beaten.*

Evander made a quick jab at him, pleased when the prince swung his crude practice sword in a tight arch, knocking aside the blow. He followed immediately, pivoting towards him and swinging at him. Evander leaned back to avoid it, stepping backwards into his own shadow and letting himself fall, sinking into it and immediately coming out in Caiden's shadow.

His weapon prodded at the prince's back. "Dead."

Caiden glared at him. "I'm starting to think you have an unfair advantage."

Evander grinned. "You need to learn to fight ability users. Granted, I can see how mine might be a pain."

"A pain? You disappear! You can pop up fifty paces off, or you could be right behind me!"

"Then try to predict where I'm going." He paused. Something about that struck him as important, an odd feeling that he'd missed something. He shrugged it off as Caiden demanded a rematch. Again.

Evander was happy to oblige. While the practice swords were nothing more than a couple of clumsily carved sticks, he'd taken care to make them slightly heavier than the metal blades that they'd acquired from the bandits. He was using the spars as a way to get accustomed to implementing his ability in combat while simultaneously training Caiden. With frequent use, it was becoming more powerful. He'd always been able to manipulate shadows but now he could give it form, separate it, and give the illusion of a phantom. He'd begun using it to recreate the elite's abilities for Caiden to practice against. Not that it was anything close to the real thing. He was concerned, however.

Over the past week, the prince had been keeping his distance from him and their spars were getting increasingly violent. They hadn't argued save for directly after the fight with the bandits, and Evander wondered if Caiden was still upset over it.

*"What are you doing?"* Evander asked as he stripped the last of the equipment from the body in front of him. He'd turned around to see that Caiden had arranged the bodies and seemed to be looking for something.

*"Looking for kindling. The least we can do is give them a decent send off."*

*Evander stared at him. "Smoke will attract people. Just leave them."*

*"Then at least a burial—"*

*"Why? Leave them out and they'll attract animals that we can then hunt and eat ourselves."*

*"It's basic human decency!" Caiden snapped at him, sounding horrified.*

*Evander rolled his eyes and grabbed a larger rock, using it to carve out a space in the mud.*

*"That's too shallow," Caiden said slowly.*

*"If you want to bury them, fine. Throw some dirt on them, say a prayer, and leave it be. That should be enough to satisfy you, right?" He wasn't gentle about it. Caiden would at least understand the logic behind his words, even if he didn't like them. "Come hunt here in a few days and we might be able to survive the winter."*

That had shocked Caiden into sullen silence for a while. It wasn't until Evander had started training him that he realized that the prince was still upset over something. It wasn't like him to hold a grudge, so whatever it was bothered him deeply.

He decided to wait for Caiden to make the first move in this round and was surprised when the man came at him with fury. He ended up on the defensive, redirecting blows rather than trying to block them. Caiden had the advantage in height and weight, and Evander was realizing that the prince was much stronger than he'd originally thought. Helping the cook knead bread, the physician lift bodies and grind herbs, and helping the servants run errands all had clearly given the man a good bit of muscle. What impressed him was that Caiden knew what to do with his body. He was nowhere near the clan's caliber but for someone with no true combat experience, he was showing great improvement.

Caiden was slashing at him with a viciousness that Evander hadn't known the man was capable of. The prince wasn't holding back and was truly trying to hit him.

Finally, Evander dropped his weapon and punched the prince in the chest. The blow put a fast stop to the man's forward momentum and Evander took advantage of his loss of balance. He punched again, this time in the stomach, and watched Caiden hunch over. It didn't take much effort to drive the other's face down into his knee.

Caiden reeled backwards with a yelp, landing with a solid thud on the ground. He stared up at him in shock, his nose bloodied and eyes teary from pain.

"What the hell is your problem?" Evander snapped at him. "This is to get you combat ready, not so you can take out whatever issues you have on me."

Caiden glared at him. "If you've been able to beat me, why haven't you?"

"I have been beating you. I just haven't punched you in the face. I still can if you're not satisfied yet." Caiden didn't reply and with some effort, Evander reigned in his temper. "I hold back so you can learn more. I still beat you and I hurt you to some extent so you will learn faster, but there's no reason for me to come at you without restraint. You, on the other hand, wanted to hurt me. Why?"

Caiden dropped his gaze then. "You killed a retreating woman."

Evander stared at him. "And?" *Was that really it?*

The prince's head shot up, his expression one of complete disbelief. "You killed someone in cold blood who was already retreating!"

Evander tilted his head to the side and crossed his arms over his chest. Clearly something that was common sense to him was not making sense to Caiden. "Had she gotten away she would have told someone. She could have come back with reinforcements or she could have followed us. It's practically winter; we can't afford to move and find other shelter."

"We could have kept her alive!"

"With what resources? We have enough food to keep us well fed and to last perhaps two weeks into winter, but after that? We will have to find a way of stealing or otherwise acquiring food. We don't have enough excess to support a prisoner. Not to mention having to keep track of her. All in all, letting her live would have caused nothing but problems."

Caiden blinked at him for a moment and Evander could see him thinking it through. "I... understand."

The prince suddenly seemed so much younger. The lost look almost made Evander want to hit him again. "Do you really?" he asked with a raised brow.

"I... I do. Really. Sorry for going off like that."

Evander gave a nod and helped him back to his feet. "I forget you're not a killer at heart."

"I take that as a compliment," Caiden muttered.

He seemed to relax more and Evander figured that his outburst was a good thing. A gust of wind made him shiver. Now that he'd been standing still, the cold was biting into him. Not a good thing right after exercise.

He began a quick round of stretches, even going so far as to settle on his back on the ground and arching into a bridge. Caiden gave him a curious look before shaking his head and starting to walk away from him.

"Stretch," he called as he relaxed again.

The prince turned back to glare at him.

"I'm serious. Stretch." Evander sat up and stretched his arms out before bending to touch his feet, his chest laying against his legs.

"I can't do that." Caiden was watching him with a combination of awe and concern. "I have no idea how you do that."

"I'm not telling you to do as I do. I'm just saying you need to stretch out your muscles. Believe me, everyone above the age of ten in the clan is faster, more flexible, more acrobatic, and far more capable than you are. Your best bet is to at least try and catch up."

"Well, that's comforting," Caiden muttered sullenly. Yet Evander watched as the man started mimicking him, or attempting to. After a few minutes of the Prince struggling to touch his toes without bending his knees and slowly working the tightness out of his shoulders, the man picked up his bow and quiver. "I'm going to hunt. We're running low on food."

Evander found himself rolling his eyes, but he got to his feet and wandered over to the clothesline and buckets that they were using for laundry. He was almost back to full strength, though Caiden was still leery of letting him overwork himself, a funny thing considering how wholeheartedly Caiden had thrown himself into training. The man had basically confined him to the cabin, showing him how to oil and work the skins that he'd stretched to keep them supple. Showing him how to do laundry, and to properly cook a meal.

Evander sighed and grumbled to himself as he pulled the sheets off of the line. He could sew a button, but he didn't know how to mend a tear. He could apply a bandage but couldn't disinfect a wound. He could kill but couldn't hunt. He could organize a full meal with all the necessary nutrients but had no idea how to cook it. He knew how to quickly wash a shirt but had no idea how to wash and dry full loads of laundry.

He threw the now-dry linens into the basket. They'd managed to find the bandit's camp, so they had more clothes and supplies.

"You seem to have gotten used to doing laundry, at least."

Evander glared over his shoulder at Caiden as the man laughed and headed off into the woods. He continued with the chores, pacing around and cleaning. Reorganizing, so they could run if necessary. Paranoid, he knew, but it was better to be prepared.

They'd gained armor from the bandits, though none of it fit either of them and most of it was rotted or so crusted over with blood and gore that it was practically unusable. So, Evander had torn it all apart and started piecing it back together into what he hoped would be at least a half-decent set of armor for each of them. His own was ruined by all the blood and Caiden hadn't known how to properly clean or treat the armor—or it just wasn't his priority, Evander couldn't tell which. He still had a few pieces that were usable though.

He occupied his time trying to layer and stitch a chest piece. Even though he was working carefully. he could tell it was going to be mediocre work at best... if he were honest, it was even less than that. Downright pathetic.

Caiden was usually quick with his hunts, going out to check his traps and kill what he could before coming back. Evander paced some more before going to fetch water from the nearby stream. He used his ability to get there and used his injured arm to carry it back. His own way of exercising outside of their usual sparing.

He sighed as he returned to the cabin, setting the water down by the hearth before stretching out his arms again. It had been almost a month since they'd escape the castle, thirty-one days to be exact, so long as Caiden was correct in his count of days. Judging by the stars, he'd say the prince wasn't mistaken. The constellation of the Maiden had risen in the night sky only twelve days prior.

The funerals would have taken place already. Messages would have been sent to the neighboring kingdoms. Border patrols and search parties would have formed. Evander wondered if Ansom had replaced Caiden's body to make it look like the prince was dead.

He promptly discarded the idea. No, the easiest way to keep up his charade was if he had the whole kingdom to find and bring the prince to him. Once he had him, it would be simple to stage an accident.

He shrugged off the thoughts and decided to clean, only pausing when it began to get dark. He frowned at the fire, tapping his foot against the floorboards. Caiden almost always returned as the sun set. He was late. He paced for a few moments more before grabbing his sword and heading outside.

He froze only three steps out of the door, spotting a light moving through the trees.

He activated his ability, pulling the darkness around him until he was practically invisible in the night. Skulking towards the path, he kept low, staying near the brush. His stomach did a small flip as he caught sight of an old man slowly making his way down the path. He was laden with packs, hobbling along while holding out a lantern.

The owner of the cabin was early. Most likely to start stocking for the winter months that would be spent there. Evander drew his sword and waited. The man got to the clearing and Evander could see his confusion, his trepidation, as he saw the light of the fire through the windows. The man cautiously moved forward, raising his lantern higher as he approached the door.

Evander slid behind him with the ease of a practiced killer, raising his sword at an angle to plunge into the man's side. An easy kill. A necessary one. Caiden may not like it, but they couldn't afford for anyone to find them, not now.

The man paused at the door and Evander took a breath—

"Excuse me, Sir?"

Evander mentally cursed, diving to the side, using a shadow to put himself close to the cabin wall as the elder whipped around. Caiden stood just a few yards away, a doe dragging behind him.

The man wheezed and for a moment, Evander was sure he was going to die of shock.

"What-what in the—? What're you—? What do you think you're doin' here?"

Caiden smiled at him as he came closer. "Apologies, we needed a place to stay." He stepped into the light cast by the man's lantern.

"You-Your Highness!" The man tried to bow, almost falling over as his packs weighed him down. "I-I'm honored, bu— How?"

Caiden reached out to steady him, and the man finally let out a wheezing chuckle. "I think I need a drink."

Caiden maintained his smile, his gaze sliding to where Evander stood. The prince gave a slight shake of his head and Evander sighed, releasing his ability and sheathing the sword. The man jumped.

"You! You're that-that assassin everyone's been— Your Highness, please stay back!"

Evander tilted his head to the side and watched as the old man positioned himself in front of the prince.

Even so the elder was shaking from head to toe, eyes wide and clearly terrified.

Caiden put his hand on the man's shoulder. "Sir, please calm down. Could you explain what's going on?"

"But—"

"He isn't going to hurt you, I promise. If you would please..." Caiden gently herded the elder into the house and Evander followed, perching on the edge of the bed and doing his best not to scare the old man.

"Well, first, please let me say it is such a blessing to see you alive and well, Your Highness," the man babbled as Caiden helped him into a chair, taking the bags from him.

"Thank you," the prince replied with a smile that made Evander roll his eyes. He had no idea how Caiden had managed to learn how to handle himself, but that was a court smile if he ever saw one. Automatic, pleasant, and completely empty.

"His Majesty's advisor has taken the throne as regent while you were gone. Waiting for your return, I'm sure. He expressed great urgency in finding you alive and bringing you home."

"I'm sure," Caiden replied dryly.

The old man didn't seem to catch on to the animosity. "He has given the search for you top priority after... well, after..." He stared fearfully at Evander.

"Why do you fear him?" Caiden asked.

"He... well, I'm sure he can't be the one since he is with you, but... his likeness is all over the Kingdom. It is said that the prince's own servant was responsible for the assassinations. Lord Ansom said that he was killed, though his body was not retrieved... We were all ordered to report anyone fitting his description."

Evander and Caiden shared a look before the prince returned his attention to the old man.

"He is the only reason I got out of the castle alive. I assure you, he has my complete confidence."

"Oh, I'm sure. Your Highness... why have you been hiding here if I may ask? I-I'm honored that you chose to stay here of course, you are very welcome, Your Highness."

Caiden sighed, and Evander could see his annoyance with being addressed in such a roundabout way. "I'm avoiding the assassin that killed my family. Do you know if there is any kind of resistance to Ansom's rule? Any survivors from the castle?"

"Well there are a few, a group of knights and some nobles."

"Do you know where they are?"

"They seem to be hiding in the Capital. I-I've only heard rumors."

"I need you to tell them where to find me. I must meet with them."

"W-well of course, Your Highness, I'd be delighted to assist."

In the end, Evander carefully helped the man store his things, trying not to scare him. He wasn't entirely successful. The elder was clearly still suspicious of him, so in the end he settled for just steering clear of the man.

They insisted that the old bat have the bed, Evander sitting up while Caiden curled up on a makeshift bed of blankets in the corner by the fire. Evander paced every once in a while, stirring the fire to keep the room relatively warm. Also, to make sure that neither of them would wake at the sound of movement. If they fell asleep to his noise, they wouldn't wake up to it.

A few hours later, he deemed Caiden deep enough into his dreams that he wouldn't notice anything amiss. He quietly picked up the dagger that they used for gutting and skinning. Caiden wasn't going to like it, but if the man said anything to anyone about where they were, Ansom's elites would be knocking on their door in less than a week. Well, they'd be breaking down the door, if they didn't just light the place on fire and watch them burn with it.

Evander couldn't remember the man's name. He didn't want to. He was still trying to bury the thought of the family that the elder had left behind. A daughter whose husband had died, with a child and an infant to care for. The smile on his wrinkled face as he recalled his grandchildren... Evander crushed the memory and tried to bury it. It had to be done. He had to protect the heir.

He looked down at the thin, frail figure, covered by thick quilts and still shivering. So weak. He flipped the dagger over in his hand, adjusting his grip.

And hesitated.

He grit his teeth, his knuckles going white over the hilt. It would only take one strike. That's all.

Painless. He wouldn't even know, wouldn't feel anything.

Evander shifted, slowly moving into a satisfying position over the sleeping elder.

Caiden would be heartbroken. *Idiot prince.*

He relaxed, silently cursing and grinding his teeth in frustration. He could only imagine that this was how the hunting dogs felt while pulling at their leashes. He turned away from the bed and silently made his way back to his seat, replacing the dagger as he'd found it.

The rustle of fabric made him turn towards Caiden, finding those blue eyes watching him before silently turning over and settling to sleep again. Not a word was spoken, and for a moment Evander was almost convinced that the man had been sleeping with his eyes open. Yet, he knew better. Caiden was too tense, too still where he lay to truly be sleeping.

Evander chewed the inside of his cheek for a moment. *Pain in the ass.*

He sat heavily at the edge of Caiden's makeshift bed, leaning into the body behind him. When the prince didn't acknowledge him, he sighed out loud and stretched out his legs, putting more of his weight into the man. When that still didn't work, he tugged at the quilt that was wrapped around him.

Finally, Caiden squirmed and shifted, unwrapping himself enough to leave some room and moving closer to the wall. Evander chuckled and they took turns pushing and prodding, pulling, and elbowing until both had settled comfortably.

Evander had no real intentions of sleeping, but he knew that Caiden would sleep soundly knowing that he didn't intend to kill the old man. That and it was cold in the cabin, especially as the fire started to die.

So, as he listened to the prince's breathing even out into sleep, Evander laid still and tried to think of how he was going to convince Caiden to move somewhere else as soon as the old hunter left. Just thinking about the task left him with a headache.

# Chapter Seven
Month of the Maiden 16, 421 HE


*A butterfly danced in front of him, the bark of the courtyard tree a solid and comfortable presence at his back. The small creature fluttered downwards and the weight in his lap shifted and squirmed.*

*He smiled and looked down at the small child that he held, tiny little hands reaching for the insect with a refreshing sense of wonder. He pressed a kiss to the matt of black hair and the toddler giggled, his head tilting back to grin up at him. Golden eyes, just like his own, sparkled with laughter.*

*"Master."*

*He turned towards the sullen sounding speaker, finding a young man standing just out of range. Another one that looked very much like himself. Black hair and eyes the color of whiskey.*

*"What may I do for you, Ansom? Has the prince escaped from you again?" he chuckled.*

*The glare he earned made him grin.*

*"Sir, he is completely unsuitable. All he ever does is run around. He isn't even prepared for his first child."*

*He sighed. "I did tell his Majesty that the arranged marriage wasn't going to be a good idea. Especially at this age."*

*"He should be prepared to inherit the throne! It's only a month away! Still, he shirks his duties!"*

*"And what would you have me do?" he smiled placatingly at the man.*

*Ansom glared at him again. "Well, for starters, you can stop playing around with the child," he spat. "We have our rules in place for a reason. Besides, how do you expect to train him into one of us if you coddle him?"*

*He looked down at the child in his arms. He was completely fascinated by the butterfly which had landed on his toes. He didn't move, didn't startle it, just watched with a restraint that was rare in a child of his age.*

*He wondered idly if Ansom was jealous. He had to admit he wasn't exactly proud of his past demeanor. His patience had been learned with age, his master's teachings losing their potency as he watched over his charge and grew older himself. He'd learned the error of his ways, but it would seem that his old bitterness had already corrupted some of their members. It was his greatest mistake.*

*His arms tightened around the child in front of him, the movement causing the object of his fascination to make a quick escape.*

*"Bye, bye, flutter!"* A tiny hand waved at the creature.

*"Come along, Evander. Let's show Ansom what you've learned today."*

*Maybe there was still time to fix this. Then again-*

Evander frowned, rubbing at his eyes as he sat up: something was weird. A sound reached his ears. A gentle tune, the quiet chime of a music box coming to an end. He threw off the blanket and jumped to his feet, attempting to locate it— A clattering sound rang out as a small wooden box fell to the floor.

His heart sank into his stomach. He slowed his breathing and held still, listening for anything amiss as he slowly turned. That box was not there when they went to sleep the night before. Caiden didn't own such a thing and it hadn't been amongst the old man's belongings that were left behind. Yet, there was no one there.

He stared down at the small, plain box.

"Eva? What're you doing?" Caiden yawned as he sat up.

He didn't answer, crouching, balancing on the balls of his feet as he slowly reached for the thing. It fit snugly in his palm and he slowly turned it over, finding the key slot to wind it but not the key.

"Eva?" Caiden leaned over to look at what he was doing. Evander looked up as the prince also froze, eyes darting around the empty cabin.

Caiden quietly got out of bed and walked to the door, shaking his head at Evander to say that the door was still bolted shut. He checked the windows with the same result, rubbing his hands over his crossed arms, shivering in the predawn chill.

Evander hummed, running his fingers over the music box. The cold was settling into his body as well and the wood felt odd under his numbed touch. "Don't bother," he muttered. "Help me find the key to this."

"Eva, what the hell is going on? How did—"

"Help me find the key!" he snapped and Caiden blinked at him, falling silent as he opened the windows to let in the early morning light.

They searched for a while, but they kept the place meticulously clean and it quickly became obvious that the key to the music box wasn't there.

"Eva, what is that thing?"

"A music box." He held it up to show the prince.

"A music box? Aren't those extremely rare? Where did it come from?"

"I don't know."

"How did someone get in here? Why did they leave it?"

"I don't know!" Evander glared at Caiden and his endless questions. "Maybe if you had listened to me when I said we have to leave then we wouldn't have to worry about it!"

"I keep telling you, what is the point of sitting around doing nothing? We need help, Eva! We need them to find us! We can't exactly go through a border checkpoint with the whole kingdom out looking for us!"

"Ansom is going to find us, not your soldiers! For all we know, he could already be—" He paused, looking down at the music box in his hand.

Music Box. The ability to tie a memory to a tune, lock it away into a box. Anyone in contact with it while it was playing would be privy to the memory. It was an exceedingly useful ability for an assassin or a spy. It had been Malik's ability.

Blink. The ability to move through the ethereal plane. It was a lot like his own, except it allowed the user to move through walls, to walk invisible through a crowd as though they were a ghost. An ability that had been gifted to a servant woman who had gone with Malik and the old king when they'd left.

"Get packed." He grabbed his bag and gear, simultaneously getting dressed and packing with a haste that made Caiden stare.

"But—"

"We need to leave. Now."

Caiden joined him and soon they were out the door with the bare minimum of what they needed to simply survive.

He stared around himself, wondering which way to go when a shining glint caught his attention. A golden bauble, a music box key, hung by a thread from a tree branch. Right next to the well-worn path that led straight back to the capital. The path they'd sent the old man down not four days ago.

Evander snatched it and shoved it into a pocket. *Fine, I get it. Quit running away, right?*

"Who—?"

"Malik. Or whoever the servant was that went with him."

"Ellen," Caiden provided.

Evander raised an eyebrow at him.

Caiden shrugged. "She was my father's nursemaid. Father was under the impression that she and Malik were married, so it wasn't a surprise when she left with him."

Evander stared at him for a moment before starting down the path.

"Wait, so wouldn't that make her your—?"

"We need to move, Caiden," Evander cut him off, moving quickly through the trees.

They kept low and Evander quietly explained his theory that the music box was functioning as a warning.

"How do you figure?" Caiden muttered, just as quiet, waiting while Evander untangled himself from a thorn bush that had snagged his clothing.

"Well," he tore himself free and stumbled off balance for a moment, "it was a memory of Ansom. I can't think of any other reason why she'd — assuming this was Ellen — would track us down and leave it there."

"Why didn't she just wake us up? That doesn't make sense. If it was that urgent, why wouldn't she just talk to us?"

"I don't know." Evander growled in frustration as he almost tripped over a branch. *What the hell?* He glared at the offending thing for a moment.

They were well beyond their usual hunting grounds and while it would be faster if he used his ability, he had no idea where they were in relation to the city and he didn't really want to run into Ansom while jumping. Something was strange though.

"Eva?" Caiden asked.

"I swear, this wasn't here a moment ago." He kicked at the branch.

Caiden frowned, turning to look back down the path where they'd come from. "And that bush doesn't naturally lie over the path. It looks like a branch was tampered with." He turned back to face him and his eyes widened, hand going to his sword, mouth opening to warn him.

Evander twisted and ducked, barely avoiding a slice to the throat. He threw himself back, away from the attacker, and felt himself snarl at the man who stood in their way. He was disgustingly familiar, tall, unnaturally thin, with ratty brown hair and a rat-like face to match, his mouth curling into a sneer.

"Oh, how the great have fallen, Evander," the newcomer chuckled, lifting his head and letting out a shrill whistle. "Though, I must admit, I'm surprised to see you alive."

"Ben," Evander growled, his skin prickling with animosity.

"I knew I should've had him killed." Caiden sounded downright murderous, and Evander felt his face heat with the knowledge that the Prince had also been aware of *that*.

"Ah, so that was you." Ben grinned. "Should've known when you banished me. Too bad. Once that order was given, I had been planning to have so much fun tormenting you to death, Evander."

*Order?* He'd always assumed that it had been part of the Harrowing. It was a hazing type ritual that encouraged the younger members of the clan to be extremely paranoid and light sleepers. Some people were never targeted, others got caught multiple times. No holds barred. If someone managed to get the jump on you, you were at their mercy. If you caught them, then you could do as you pleased with them.

*Evander swayed on his feet, his vision doubling even as everything went fuzzy and faded. He stumbled, jerking to attention just in time to intercept a strike.*

*"Stop," Ansom's command ended the practice match. There was muttering around the room as their leader came into the ring. Evander could feel himself swaying even as he tried to stand still.*

*Ansom grabbed his jaw, forcibly turning his face so he could look at him. After a moment of silence, the man let go, turning away. "Enough for today, Evander. You're dismissed."*

*Evander gave a clumsy bow and handed his wooden sword to the nearest person before stumbling to the stairs. He was so tired... so, so tired. He felt like he hadn't slept for a week.*

*Lissa was standing in the hall, waiting for him. Though she didn't say anything, she walked with him to his room. A mercy, since he may have fallen asleep in the corridor otherwise.*

*He was rarely left alone nowadays. Whether it was by coincidence or if by design, he had no idea. But the attacks only came if he was alone, so he was thankful for it. Once he was safely in bed, Lissa bid him goodnight and left.*

*He couldn't sleep. He knew he couldn't sleep. Evander sat up and cautiously examined his room. There was no one there. He thought briefly of asking to sleep in Caiden's room, but decided against it since the prince would ask too many questions.*

*Already, Caiden had noticed something was wrong. It wasn't difficult. He'd been making stupid mistakes, forgetting even the most basic of appointments. It had been a week of constant harassment.*

*He felt tears well up in his eyes, a sob stuck in his chest. He was so tired, but who could help him? This was normal. Someone would have done something otherwise. No one would help him. Under fair circumstances, he'd be able to beat whoever it was, even if there was more than one person, but somehow he never managed to catch them in time to defend himself. The attacks came out of nowhere, usually when his back was turned or when he was sleeping.*

*He should have been able to hear them.*

*Evander felt himself nodding off and, try as he might, he couldn't fight it. He collapsed into sleep.*

*Only hours later, Evander jolted out of his sleep, deep set paranoia screaming at him that something was there, even if he didn't hear anything. He threw his blankets off, towards the edge where someone might be standing. It only bought him a second in which he briefly saw the only member of the clan who could sneak up on* anyone *without being heard.*

*Ben's ability was cheating. It wasn't fair. Silent Step wasn't fair.*

*Evander couldn't move fast enough to stop the sack from being thrown over his head, his hands clawing at the cord as it tightened around his neck.*

Oh Gods, he's actually going to kill me. *He abandoned the attempt to get the thing off, striking in the direction where Ben had been standing, but the other must've moved. Evander couldn't hear him; he didn't know where he was. He guessed and lashed out, punching with one hand while trying to loosen the cord around his neck with the other.*

*Ben grabbed his wrist and he felt himself being twisted. Next thing he knew was blinding pain as he was pinned to the ground.*

*Evander yelped; the sound muffled.*

*"Shh," Ben hushed him. "Careful not to wake that prince of yours."*

*This was the first time Evander had heard him speak and it sent shudders of terror through him. Ben knew that Evander had seen him, and he didn't care to hide his identity anymore.* He's actually going to kill me. *Evander concluded as he felt rope tighten around his pinned arms. He struggled but as he tried to move his now bound arms, the cord tightened, strangling him until he returned to the uncomfortable position with his arms wrist to elbow behind his back.* Bastard. *He wanted to scream, to kick and thrash, but Ben's weight was on his legs. He couldn't move unless he wanted to strangle himself and possibly make enough noise to get the guards outside or Caiden's attention.*

*He was too tired. He couldn't breathe through the hood and his adrenaline was fading. He gasped for air that wouldn't satisfy his lungs and could do nothing but try to be quiet. He'd rather die than let Caiden see this. If anything happened, questions would be asked, the prince would have a full-blown investigation in motion and Evander couldn't risk that.*

*It was no good. His awareness was fading faster than he could think to stave it off. But what was the point of trying? He was tired anyways. He just wanted it to end.*

He'd fainted after that but when he woke, he was perfectly safe if not a bit sore, and Caiden was throwing a tantrum. The only fit he'd ever had.

The prince had demanded that Ben be brought to charge for some slight, finding every flaw, every reason to banish the man. Evander had been relieved. He was never able to sleep soundly unless Caiden was with him, but after that it seemed that no one else would dare to try again. Or maybe Ben had been the only assailant from the beginning?

Evander broke free of the memories as Ben rushed towards him, stopping short to avoid Caiden's strike and ducking down to lash out at Evander. He avoided the blade easily. Ben wasn't one of Ansom's elites. He must have been called on to act as a scout.

They had to get to an open space. It was too easy for the clan to hide amongst the trees and pick them off. They had to get rid of Ben quickly before the others caught up. It was a strange feeling, as Ben laughed at him, played with him. Underestimated him. He couldn't even bring himself to be angry. There was no need for vengeance, no feeling of anything other than a cold sense of duty.

The man in front of him wanted them dead, wanted Caiden dead. He was no longer the terror that Evander remembered. He was clumsy, slow, his strength nowhere near what it used to be. Caiden lunged at him and Ben jumped back to dodge, stiffening in shock as Evander's blade sank into his back. Evander let the man slide off of his sword, bending to grab the bandolier of throwing knives from the fallen assassin and slip it over his own head, tightening the straps.

"Caiden," he said slowly, his attention on the subtle sounds of movement through the brush.

"Evander." The reply was an easy acceptance.

Without another word, Evander surged forward with Caiden right behind him.

Evander drew a throwing knife into his hand, pulling the shadows around himself. There was a rustling as someone came towards them from the side. He threw without taking the time to properly aim and was surprised to hear the choked cry and crash of a falling body.

They were quickly approaching a clearing and he put on a burst of speed, rolling into the open a few steps before Caiden. He turned and threw another knife at the assassin who'd been waiting for them.

She cursed and dove to the side to avoid the blade, leaving Caiden clear to join him.

Ansom was known to have five favorites, referred to as his 'elites.' Kaitlyn, Connor, Max, Sarah, and Carrow. He'd quizzed Caiden on them mercilessly until the prince knew all of their abilities by heart and knew how to avoid being killed within the first minute of meeting them.

*"Kaitlyn."*

*"Catlike Reflexes. Fast, flexible, pain in the ass."*

*"Correct. How do you nullify it?"*

*"Keep her in close quarters, disable as quickly as possible."*

*"Caiden, she may look like an eleven-year-old girl, but she is vicious and she's a quick learner. You must kill her as soon as you have her. There are no second chances."*

Kaitlyn was attacking Caiden. Having already been beaten by Evander, it seemed that she had no desire to face him again. Actually, it seemed that the Elites didn't know what to do with him.

"Well, well, aren't you a surprise." Ansom's voice was steady but at a glance, Evander could see his fury. "Here I was expecting you to die a slow and painful death by poison."

Evander frowned as the Ansom's gaze darted to his men. As though to make sure they heard him, as if he had to justify his failure to kill him.

"Well, this does change things. Let me make this clear to all of you, if you fail to kill the pest, you will be considered unworthy of our clan. Am I clear?"

Evander couldn't help rolling his eyes at the collective 'Yes, sir' that came from the elites. Suddenly, he was the center of attention. He spotted four of them. Kaitlyn, Sarah, Max, and Connor, meaning that he had to have hit Carrow earlier. A lucky strike.

Kaitlyn continued to battle with Caiden, keeping the prince's attention. He was doing well, protecting his vitals and slowly coaxing her closer. It wouldn't be long before she fell into a rhythm, lulled into dropping her guard. It was a bad habit that she never grew out of and one that he'd told Caiden about in extensive detail.

The other three, however, had turned on him. He danced backwards, keeping out of range of the greatsword that Sarah swung around single handedly. Her ability had a three-foot range, and he steered himself clear of it.

"Hold up," Connor chuckled, shoving past her. "I'll take care of this one."

"Back off, I'm taking the credit on this one," she snarled at him.

"Both of you, knock it off. It doesn't matter which of us kills him so long as he's dead."

Evander stepped backwards, sinking into his own shadow as a rock was launched at his head. He came up behind Max but a floating wall of rubble had already formed, keeping him from striking.

Restless Defense. A short-ranged ability to control unattended objects. It was annoying at the best of times. He kept his debris moving, orbiting around him, making him hard to hit.

Well, two could play at that game. Evander activated his ability and pulled. The shadows gathered around him and he grinned as all three took a step back. He didn't let their shock go to waste. He drew out his daggers; sharp, wicked things that had been taken from the bandits.

He dove for Max, possibly the quickest to get rid of out of the three of them. He tended to use hand motions to direct his ability, making him a fraction too slow when he was in the middle of combat. He couldn't fight and use his ability simultaneously.

Evander pulled apart his shadows, throwing phantoms at all of them. He moved within the darkness he'd created, keeping it between the three elites, keeping them disconnected. Max moved his defenses so the rocks that he'd collected met the phantom. Evander ducked around the debris and sank his dagger into the man's side.

He disappeared into his shadows before Max fell.

"What the hell is this? You said he was useless!" Sarah screeched.

"He should be," Connor growled in response.

Evander paused at the terrified shriek that echoed through the clearing, cut short as Kaitlyn fell to Caiden's blade. He shuddered at the sound and the silence that followed.

"Dammit," Connor muttered, turning towards the prince.

"Enough of this. Dante." Ansom's voice cracked, his tone brittle, but it was the name that caught Evander's attention.

Dante was not one of the elites, however his ability was the opposite of his own, Daybreak. An ability that intensified the light in an area and made Dante himself into a light source almost on par with the sun. He was the twin brother of Lissa, the original candidate for the Princess' Guardian. Evander wanted to avoid killing him if he was able.

The boy stepped out of the tree line behind Ansom where he'd no doubt been told to hide. Evander quickly pulled everything he could with his ability until the clearing was as dark as it would be at dusk.

It only lasted a moment.

The light burned away the shadows in a matter of seconds, leaving all of them blinded. Evander didn't dare to stand still. He ran, trying to avoid the creek and failing. The splash alerted the others to his location. He dove forward, trying to force his eyes to adjust to the light.

The shadows were small now, but they were still there. When he was younger, his ability less potent, he would have been rendered helpless by this. Now, he didn't even have the chance to wonder if it would work as he saw a shadow behind Dante. He grabbed for his own, tiny though it was, and he pulled, forcing it open. He opened it beneath his own feet, dropping into the darkness.

There was no exit. It felt like he'd hit a wall. The air was being squeezed from his lungs. His body felt crushed, but he could *feel* the space he was now trapped in. He forced his eyes open and stared at the colors that danced and flickered around him. He peered at the nearest of them and could see Sarah and Connor trying to find him while also trying to save their vision.

His lungs began to burn with the need for air and he quickly found the spot that he wanted and reached out his hand. His fingers passed through the narrow opening without resistance, but he knew he wouldn't be able to fit. Then he had a sudden thought and activated his ability, expanding the opening until he could pull himself through.

He gasped for air as he dragged himself up onto solid ground but didn't give himself time to rest. He'd used the shadow of a tree to get behind Ansom and Dante. He sprinted towards them and while Ansom immediately began to move, Dante was too slow.

Evander felt the blade of his dagger meet the younger's side, the resistance and final give of cloth and flesh. Too shallow to kill, but enough for the boy to understand the warning. Then he was throwing himself away from them, not daring to try for Ansom as the light suddenly died. He jumped into the nearest shadow, aiming for the spot in front of Connor.

The other assassin saw him dive and turned to face the shadows behind him, turning his back to where Evander was aiming.

"Connor is... simple."

"You said his ability was 'Quick Step'?"

"Yep."

"So, wouldn't that make him the worst?"

"No, the worst is Kaitlyn. Her's is all skill. There's no shortcut to beating her."

"And there is a shortcut to someone with superhuman speed?" Caiden scoffed.

"His isn't speed. He slows everything down around him."

"He what?"

"I realized it a while ago. During training, he's a cocky bastard at the best of times. He plays with his kills, taunts them. He has to deactivate his ability in order to talk or be visible. He also can't keep it activated for too long."

"And how did you make this connection to his having a slow time ability?"

Evander raised an eyebrow at him. "Because someone who simply moves at superhuman speed wouldn't have to deactivate his ability just to talk."

"Okay, so how do we beat that?"

"Predict where he is going to be. Or just hit him when he pauses to talk. He never has to think, he doesn't have to react to anyone because he always makes the first move. It makes him almost easy."

Sarah had moved towards Caiden and the man was trying to stay well away from her. She was small, but covered head to toe in plate armor that would have made even the strongest man clumsy.

Evander made a quick decision and ran towards her, purposely making enough noise for Connor to realize he was there. He was prepared for it, but it still hurt when the blade skidded across his back and side, a light blow that clearly wasn't meant to kill him.

He stopped a few feet outside of Sarah's range and turned, watching Connor appear in front of him. The man was grinning.

"Y'know, this is sad. Like, I get it that the Master wants you dead and all, but this isn't even a challenge. Sure, you have some tricks up your sleeve but, hey," he shrugged, "it won't help you against me and you know it."

Evander could see it in the way the man's muscles twitched ever so slightly. He was prepared to activate his ability. He grinned, not bothering with a retort as he stabbed out with his left hand. While almost simultaneously punching out with his right. Right into the man's face.

A startled yelp met the blow and Connor reeled backwards straight into Sarah's range. The assassin hit the ground swearing, unable to move as everything became unbearably heavy.

Sarah turned, confused. "What the hell?"

Evander watched her furiously swear at the man who'd gotten caught in her ability, but it seemed she didn't care to move and free him of it. Or deactivate it, for that matter.

*That is irritating.* But it wasn't the end of his plans. He'd been hoping that she would release Connor and they'd have a chance to get to her before she could use her ability again. Evander had almost forgotten the fatal flaw of the Elites, the same flaw that was allowing him and Caiden to beat them. They weren't working together. They couldn't care less about what happened to the others. It was going to be what got them all killed.

"I'll do it myself, you useless ingrate!" she snarled and turned towards him, leaving Caiden completely unopposed. Evander backed up, letting her come closer.

"Wait, no! Sarah!" Connor's yelling became more frantic as she stepped over him. "Sarah! Sarah, stop! NO!" His screaming came to a sudden end as Sarah continued towards Evander, leaving Connor helpless in her range until Caiden was able to kill him without exposing himself to her ability as well.

Evander knew what was coming next, saw her gaze slide to the side just before she leaped backwards, trying to catch Caiden before the prince could move away.

*"She's like a spider, Caiden. Her ability is like a web. Once she catches you in it, it's over."* Evander *manipulated the shadows around him to make a circle around his feet, roughly the size of Sarah's range.*

*"Alright, so how do we beat this 'Weighted Air'?"*

*"It has a three-foot radius around her,"* Evander gestured to the darkness around him. *"Everything touching her is as light as a feather while everything else becomes weighed down to the point where you can't move. It's one of the reasons she uses a greatsword and heavy armor. It's best to use ranged attacks but with the armor, your aim has to be impeccable. Even I wouldn't be able to hit her easily. However, she isn't trained very well at all. She knows how to dodge projectiles well enough but for the most part, she just incapacitates her victims and kills them while they're trapped."*

*"Okay, so how do we get close enough to hit her?"*

*Evander smirked.*

Evander ran towards her, watching her attention snap back to him before she had completed her plan to trap Caiden. She stopped a step short and changed direction as he tried to circumvent her range.

Evander saw her grin as his foot stuck and held, his leg becoming too heavy to move. She took another step and his knees buckled as the air became thick and heavy. It felt as though he were being crushed by some huge invisible force that was pushing down on him, dragging him to the ground.

He managed to brace himself, refusing to be forced face-first into the dirt. Sarah was cackling, raising her greatsword in preparation to bring it down on his head. He nearly laughed himself. She was completely unaware of anything else around her.

The breath whooshed out of him as a weight landed on his back, using him as a step stool. Caiden vaulted himself towards the girl, grabbing her arm, the sword coming down a few inches above Evander's head. The momentum sent them both backwards, freeing Evander from Sarah's ability.

He jumped to his feet, watching as Caiden grappled the girl who now stumbled off-balance, her sword useless as Caiden held onto her wrist with one hand while tearing at her armor with the other.

Evander drew out a throwing knife as the girl flailed about, trying desperately to throw Caiden off. The moment her armor came free, he threw. He was only slightly off because of the way she was moving, the blade hitting her helmet and falling against her shoulder. Caiden grabbed for the weapon, plunging it into the newly exposed skin of her neck.

The girl shuddered and stumbled, her ability deactivating. Now weighed down by her equipment, she fell.

Evander barely had time to register their victory as he saw Ansom, kneeling by Kaitlyn's body, with a look of complete fury and disbelief on his face. As though he truly could not comprehend his failure. Then the man drew out a knife and Evander dove through the nearest shadow, coming up behind Caiden and grabbing him before throwing them both to the side, barely avoiding the blade.

Evander pulled them through another shadow, keeping a firm grip on Caiden, keeping them low for a fraction longer than what was natural. There was a whoosh of air as another knife sailed over their heads. Even as he missed, Ansom was in the process of throwing another one. Evander stepped backwards into his own shadow, aiming for the tree line.

He yelped as he was met with a dagger sliding past his arm.

They couldn't win like this, not on the defensive. He dove again, falling into another shadow as he was released from the last.

*Heh. Should've called my ability Tactical Retreat.* He chuckled breathlessly, listening to Ansom's roar of frustration quickly getting fainter as they made their escape.

# Chapter Eight
Month of the Maiden 16, 421 HE

Evander tried to place Caiden down rather than simply dropping him. However, he wasn't entirely successful seeing as he was also in the process of falling. Both laid still, panting and groaning in pain as the aftereffects of his ability made themselves known. More so for Caiden but, while he wasn't retching, Evander felt like he'd been trampled by a horse.

"Ugh... think we lost him...?" Caiden asked slowly as he sat up, wiping his mouth on his sleeve.

Evander groaned as he pushed himself upright. "I think... we're okay... for now." He winced as he got to his feet. "We have to move... Where are we?"

Both of them stared around themselves. The trees were thinner, and the mountains were startlingly close.

"Did you take us inland?"

"Well, I didn't want to hit the ocean and have nowhere to go. Still, I'm not entirely sure where we ended up. I was hoping we'd be closer to the Capital."

Caiden huffed out a laugh. "Well, we are certainly nowhere near the city. We're too far south."

"Go west."

Both men drew their weapons and spun, trying to find the source of the unfamiliar voice.

There was no one there. Evander and Caiden shared a look.

"Please tell me you heard it too?" Caiden asked.

"I was really hoping I was imagining it," Evander muttered, slowly turning in a circle.

"Oh, sorry about that. Over here, dear."

Both of them stared at the woman who wavered into view. She seemed ethereal, dark brown hair curling ever so slightly around her face where it had escaped its tie, large brown eyes of a hue that, as the sunlight struck her features, glimmered with a vibrant shade of amber. She had a sweet, honey tone to her skin and she smiled as they continued to stare.

Evander found himself speechless but as Caiden looked between the two of them, the Prince finally broke the silence.

"Well, damn. Guess we know where you got your looks," he laughed.

Evander blinked at him then back at the woman. "You're Ellen?"

The woman gave a single nod, watching him closely.

"Care to explain what's going on?" he asked, letting his suspicion seep heavily into his voice.

It made her grin.

"Hey, Eva, that's no way to talk to—"

"I'm not in any condition to do anything at the moment. Even now I'm struggling to keep a physical form," Ellen cut Caiden off. "Though I do apologize that I had to resort to such roundabout methods."

"What's to the west?" Evander continued his questioning.

"Shores Pass villa. It is where we are currently staying. I thought I'd extend an invitation since you clearly need to rest and heal." She looked down to his side and Evander finally paused to examine himself.

His side was bloody from Connor's strike and he could feel the shallow cut where it extended around to his back. It wasn't deep, but it hurt and it would hinder his movement unless he got it treated. That wasn't even accounting for any infection that might set in if he let it be.

"Not to mention you don't seem to have any supplies," she added.

Evander quickly took stock of what they had. He wanted to smack himself. They'd dropped their heavier packs when they started fighting. They had no blankets, no clothes, no food, no tools. He sighed irritably. They still had the satchel that Caiden carried. It had the music box, some medical herbs, and supplies. Other than that, they weren't going to be able to survive for very long in the wilds, not going into a cold autumn.

Ellen's form flickered and became almost transparent. "Be sure you aren't followed," was all she said before she disappeared.

Evander looked around, throwing his hands in the air with frustration when she was nowhere to be found.

"So, to the coast?" Caiden asked slowly.

Evander turned to look at him, finding that while he was the one suggesting it, Caiden looked more queasy than anything else at the idea.

Evander chuckled and held out his hand. "That way, right?" he asked, pointing.

"Yep."

--†--

By the time they arrived at the mountainous, coastal villa, both of them were exhausted. It hadn't taken them long. A matter of hours rather than days, even with the multiple stops that they had to take to rest. However, it took its toll on their bodies.

Caiden practically had to carry Evander to the door.

"I thought... this place was... abandoned..." Evander slurred, resting his forehead against the back of Caiden's shoulder. His head was pounding and his limbs were completely useless with fatigue.

"I thought so too. Most of the royal palaces and villas were torn down or abandoned when my great grandfather took the throne. He deemed them 'unnecessary excess'."

"Mm. Wasn't that after several generations of rulers wanting their own palaces designed to their liking?"

"That's true. So, I suppose he was right." Caiden sighed and shifted, keeping Evander firmly on his back while he walked up to the main doors and pulled the bell string.

It was quiet for a few minutes. Evander lifted his head and squinted up at the building. It was a simple yet beautiful structure nestled in the mountains on a cliffside with a clear view of the sea and the port city sprawled at its base. Large windows ensured constant sunlight during the day, but it was small with only two floors. The lower for entertaining guests and the upper for bedrooms. At least, that's as far as Evander's knowledge went. It was the same design as the villa where the Queen spent most of her time. Finally, a voice could be heard on the other side of the thick wood, bolts and chains clanking together as it was unlocked.

"Ellen, for the love of all that is holy in this world, I told you not to go getting involved with—"

An older man in his upper sixties or early seventies opened the door and stared at them. He was tall, solidly built but lean, his hair, tied back in a low tail, was black streaked heavily with grey, and his eyes were an amber brown. Malik Vladimir glared at them.

"Were you followed?"

"Uh, I don't think that's possible," Caiden said slowly as he let Evander down.

"Good. Then, however you got here, do the same to get back to wherever you came from. I am not getting involved."

They both stared as the man slammed the door and relocked it. Then they listened as the chains rattled again and the door swung open with seemingly no one attending it.

"Ignore him. Come inside before you freeze." Ellen's voice was a soft whisper though she was nowhere to be seen.

"Um, thanks?" Caiden stepped inside, having to support most of Evander's weight. The door closed, and the chains and bolts were struck home by invisible hands.

"I don't think I will ever get used to that." Caiden muttered airily.

The entry of the house was beautifully crafted. The mahogany staircase wound upwards from the side, leading to the upper balcony. The banister was carved with painstaking detail. Straight back could be seen the kitchens and the room to the right seemed to be some sort of drawing room, judging by the desk. To the left was a large dining room. Evander couldn't see the interior very well. The only light was coming from a few candles in the entryway, kitchen, and the archway that lead to the room farther down on the right.

Voices could be heard from that room, and both men shared a questioning glance before moving towards it.

"Malik, who was that? You know we rarely get visitors!"

"Your Highness, it was no one of importance. I've already sent them away."

"Preposterous! Rude! Malik, you should know better! I'm bored, damn you!"

"Stop throwing a tantrum before you throw out your back again!" Malik's voice snapped.

They both paused to peek around the corner of the archway, seeing that whatever the room had been before, it was now converted into a bedroom. A large fire was roaring in the fireplace, a bed had been set up to the side, and tapestries, rugs, and furs were spread over the floors and walls to retain the heat. A pair of cushioned chairs sat in front of the fireplace, one of which held a frail old man, his hair thin and grey.

Malik stood behind the other chair, clearly at ease bantering with the man. Evander found himself staring at the scene. It was such a simple thing, so natural. Malik leaned against the chair, smiling at the elderly man, patiently listening to his griping. Then Caiden stepped out and Evander could see the training kick in as Malik turned to assess the 'threat'.

He frowned when he saw it was Caiden, and it was only then that Evander realized he'd activated his ability without thinking. He let go of the shadows that he'd gathered as he stepped out beside the prince.

"I thought I locked the door."

"You did." Ellen's voice was a clear challenge, as though she was daring him to refute her decision to let them in.

The man rolled his eyes, "Did you get stuck again?"

There was no reply and he sighed. The old King, on the other hand, was struggling to look around.

"Malik, I thought you said we didn't have guests?"

"They've decided to invite themselves in. Well?" He glared at them and gestured for them to come forward. "Introduce yourselves to your host."

"Malik, stop being rude. I almost forgot you used to run my court."

"Apologies, Your Highness, however I dislike intruders."

"Nonsense, they are guests now. Is that wee little Caiden I see?" The old man laughed and beckoned the prince forward. "My, you've grown, I haven't seen you since you were only to my knee. You look just like your father." The old king opened his arms, tears welling in his eyes though he didn't cry.

Caiden swallowed, and Evander could see the sudden strain on the man. He realized they hadn't talked much about Caiden's family since the day he woke up. Caiden had been mourning silently and alone, or perhaps he hadn't come to terms with it at all.

Malik watched the exchange with unhidden suspicion as Caiden came within the old man's reach. Wrinkled hands welcomed him, and Caiden smiled as the elder insisted on giving him a hug.

"It must have been hard. It's alright now, they won't find you here." The elder squeezed his arms tightly around Caiden and Evander could see the prince's back shudder in a silent sob.

Malik frowned. "Your Highness, what are you—?"

"I'm old, Malik. I may be sick but I'm not deaf. I heard the bells, just as you did." The man sighed as Malik made a noise of frustration. "Really, I'm no child. You didn't have to protect me from the news." Still he held Caiden, withered hands stroking and patting, eyes glistening.

"I was going to tell you."

"I know. But now you owe me a boon." The old man grinned over Caiden's shoulder, and Malik visibly recoiled from the idea.

"What do you want?"

"The key to the Music Room." The elder released the Prince, letting him wipe his eyes and step away.

"Your Highness…"

"It's not just for my sake, Malik. I will return it when they leave, I promise."

Malik sighed and slowly pulled a chain from around his neck, a simple key glinting in the firelight. Instead of handing it to the old King, he held it out to Caiden. "Don't let him get lost in there, and please be careful."

Caiden slowly took the key with a slight frown, still scrubbing the evidence of his tears away.

"It's the second door on the left upstairs," Malik provided. "Oh, and since my darling wife decided to steal one, kindly return it to its shelf. It should be labeled."

They watched as Caiden looped the key around his neck and helped his grandfather out of the chair he'd been sitting in. Evander tilted his head as they came into view.

The old man's right leg was crippled. Not by any war injury, but his joints were stiff and swollen by illness. Lockjoint was not a kind disease by any means and it explained why a man who was no more than sixty-seven years of age would appear so much older.

Evander stepped out of the way as they walked past, about to follow after them, but a pointed look from Malik kept him still. They waited in silence until they heard the royalty reach the top of the stairs, the telltale sound of a door opening and the voices becoming muffled as they entered the new room.

"Do you have any idea the risk you've taken, bringing him here?" Malik growled.

Evander stared at him, feeling his temper rise at the hostile tone. His head was pounding to the point he could barely see, his side was damp and cold where his blood had pasted his shirt to his skin, and he felt as though it was taking all of his effort just to keep standing.

Even so, he straightened, looked the man in the eye and with a cheery, off-handed tone replied, "I'll have you know that I was invited."

Malik stared at him for a moment before finally deflating, chuckling under his breath as he walked past him. "Gods, you really do take after me."

Evander blinked at the change of temperament, belatedly following him into the kitchen.

"I will say I was surprised to hear you were chosen to be the heir's counterpart. You were always such a small, skittish thing. When did your ability manifest? None of my reports were clear on that." He began rifling through cabinets.

"I was almost eleven," Evander replied, watching a bowl, pestle, and bandages appear.

Malik gave a low whistle. "Here I thought I was a late bloomer. Mine came when I was seven. So, what can you do, 'Shadow Dancer'?" He was pulling out jars, quickly creating some sort of paste.

"I'm sorry?"

"I'm asking what you can do. I have reports — take off your shirt and take a seat — but every single one of them says the same thing. That you've been deemed useless, worthless to the clan. Yet, here you stand, still very much alive despite my dear apprentice's best efforts." The man snorted his contempt as he finished his concoction and turned towards him.

Evander had followed his order, sitting on a nearby stool. He watched him curiously as he examined the wound, still ranting.

"That narcissism of his was always his downfall. Unfortunately, he was always a quick study. He always completed what he said he would and was never proven wrong."

Evander winced as the paste was slathered on the cut. "Who was your contact?" he asked, though he already had a sneaking suspicion.

"Soul Swap," Malik replied, eyeing the wound, "How did you get this cut?"

"That would explain her fallout with Ansom if she was keeping in contact with you. We ran into

Ansom's elites — his favorites. One was an overconfident idiot."

"He had poison on his blade then." There was a note of concern in his voice and it made Evander relax.

"If I'm still not feeling it then it's a type that I'm immune to."

Malik hummed as he wrapped the bandage around his waist. "There. Wash the gunk off tomorrow and let it scab over. It's not deep so you shouldn't have any problems once it's no longer open." He began washing out his supplies and putting them away. "You never answered my question. What can you do?"

"Nothing much. I just manipulate shadow, I can... teleport between them." He shrugged, rubbing at his face.

"That's... odd, usually abilities aren't so versatile." Malik examined him with a critical eye. "Come with me."

It was a command and Evander willingly followed the man to what he had thought was a drawing room. Much like the room next to it, it had been converted into a bedroom though it was much more simplistic. Malik walked over to the fireplace and threw a few logs in, starting a flame with practiced ease.

"Sleep. I refuse to test you when you're practically falling over." He left without another word and Evander sat heavily on the bed. He knew he was safe, but that didn't stop the paranoia. Even so, he was exhausted, and his body moved sluggishly as he crawled under the blankets.

# Chapter Nine
Month of the Maiden 17, 421 HE

Evander woke in a daze. Sunlight and salt air drifted through the broad windows, the sound of waves and sea birds a gentle call. There was warmth and steady rise and fall of Caiden's back against his own, something he had grown accustomed to after spending so long sharing a space with the prince.

He laid there for a moment, letting himself just breathe for the first time in what felt like a long time. There was something bothering him. He was sure that he'd dreamt something odd, yet it felt so real that he was trying to remember exactly what it was that bothered him so much. He'd heard voices, familiar yet... not. Felt the touch of warm, gentle hands on his face, the ghostly press of lips against his forehead.

*I love you, we missed you, thank the gods you're alive, we love you so much.*

Words that had run together in his tired mind. He wasn't sure who spoke them or if it was real or just a whimsical dream. But then Evander remembered another memory that he knew was very real from his childhood. A large hand patting his head and the statement that a parent was a parent, how nothing would change that.

Evander smiled then, turning so he could look at Caiden. It was a nice feeling, and one that he wished he'd had the sense to give his prince. He'd never actually used words to show his care for Caiden, never just hugged him for no other reason than because he wanted to. It had always been his duty. Children would die or go crazy if they didn't receive enough physical contact. Evander had never liked Caiden, had resented him for taking away what freedom he would have had as a normal servant. Over time, he'd come to love his work. Even if he didn't like the man he served, he recognized that he was at least good at heart. Now he was aware that he actually liked the prince. He'd even dare to say he loved him, in his own reserved way. Even if he didn't want to admit it to himself, Caiden had become his closest friend.

Slowly, Evander hugged Caiden, something he hadn't done in too long. There was no reason for it, but Evander silently apologized. For not taking the time to grieve, to talk. He hadn't offered even the most basic gesture of comfort. For all the terror and guilt that must have piled up, and still Caiden had only had one outburst over someone else's misfortune, not his own. His Kingdom, his birthright, was being stripped from him. He was living a life he wasn't prepared for, and all the while Evander had done nothing but train him and hammer into his head that Caiden would have to kill people to survive.

His arm tightened around the prince; his forehead pressed to Caiden's back. It was surprisingly comfortable. Evander wasn't used to showing or receiving affection. He wished he'd done so more often now. He was startled when Caiden suddenly shifted and nestled into the blankets, closer now. He looked helpless in his sleep, and Evander bit his lip to keep from laughing. The prince didn't wake when he moved, and he was sure to keep the blanket over the man so the cold wouldn't get to him.

The house was quiet. He silently padded barefoot to the kitchen and slowly unwound the bandage. He took his time cleaning the wound, doing his best to wash off the worst of the grime from his skin. He hadn't realized the condition they were in. Fighting, rolling about in the dirt, running, they had to be filthy.

"Let that air out."

He jumped, his dagger in his hand before he realized that it was Malik who'd entered the room. The man was looking around the suddenly dark kitchen with a sense of curiosity, and Evander sighed as he released his ability.

"Sorry," he muttered, returning to his task of patting his skin dry.

"Nothing to be sorry for." Malik hummed, stirring up the kitchen fire and transferring a few burning pieces to the stove. He then placed a kettle on the stovetop, turning to pull out the tools and ingredients he needed to make breakfast. "There is a new shirt for you in that room. I was surprised to find you awake. The injured should rest."

"There's no such thing as rest in our work," Evander muttered. "Besides, I've always been a light sleeper."

"Another fault of Ansom's. He sleeps sparingly, especially if he is focused on something."

Evander looked over at the man, storing the information. "How are we supposed to beat him?" he asked quietly.

"Well, first I'd like to see what you can do. Follow me." Malik set down the eggs in his hand and gestured for him to follow.

Evander did as he was asked, ducking into the room he'd borrowed to grab the shirt and pull it over his head. Malik was broader than he was, but it was a close enough fit. He then wandered into what he had originally thought was a dining room.

It was possibly the largest room in the building but, save for weapon racks and a few other pieces of equipment, it was completely empty. He instinctively caught the practice dagger that was thrown at him.

"What is this?" he asked cautiously as he came to stand in front of the older man.

"A test. I want to see what you can do." He wielded his own pair of daggers, though his set had a sharper curve than the ones given to Evander.

"You want me to fight you?" Evander asked incredulously.

Malik smirked and gave a single nod. "I can't tell you how to defeat someone of Ansom's caliber without knowing how you fight."

Evander sighed, settling into a fighting stance, letting his feet roam. Malik mirrored him. It quickly became apparent that Malik was not going to make the first move but just as Evander was about to launch into the offensive, Malik darted forward.

Only, the man weaved like a snake, able to throw his weight against a step so his body moved one way while his momentum carried him in the other. Evander saw where he would strike only a moment before it happened.

He braced against the blow, hardly having time to absorb the impact before he had to force himself to block the second dagger that came close to catching his side. The man may have been over twice his age, but he was still strong and just as fast.

They remained locked, each trying to figure out how to disengage without provoking a follow-up attack. Finally, Evander activated his ability, pushed until Malik's back was to the windows and his shadow fell upon him, and let it absorb him.

He put himself a few paces away from the man but kept the shadows that he'd pulled. Malik grinned, coming at him again, so Evander began to dance. Wrapped in darkness, he easily evaded the man but couldn't quite land a hit.

Something was wrong. It was a sudden chill down his spin and the whisper of motion that bade him to move.

Evander twisted, barely avoiding a stab to the back as Ellen joined the fight. Her blows came from thin air as she and her knives remained invisible with her ability active. Between her and Malik, he was finding himself pushed to the limit just trying to avoid the blows.

He had to rely on the speed of his reactions, his ability to twist and manipulate his body to avoid getting hit. It was reaching the point where he could barely keep track of them, split second decisions and instinct serving him better than thinking.

Finally, he allowed one of the unseen blows to fall and grabbed for the wielder. Ellen flickered into view, her face a mask of surprise as he practically threw her into Malik. He made use of the distraction, sinking into a shadow and rising just to the side of Malik where his shadow had been splintered off by the lighting.

He was met by a hard smack of the wooden dagger hitting his head. He sat, rubbing the spot and staring up at the pair. Malik didn't say anything, only offering a hand.

"Sorry." Evander apologized looking towards Ellen who was examining and flexing her wrist.

"Oh, this is nothing, dear. Actually, I'm impressed you thought to do that."

"Tell me," Malik drew his attention again, "why did you choose to come up there?" He gestured to the spot Evander had appeared from.

Evander frowned. "Because it would be too obvious if I came up directly behind you."

"I know." Malik gave him a patient smile, waiting for him to understand.

Then it clicked. The knife that sailed over his head, the one that was only a few inches off, the *order* to ostracize him. Ansom had ordered that. Why? Why would Impeccable Aim miss? Why would there be an order to kill him?

The answer was simple. Because if he used his ability, Ansom wouldn't be able to hit him.

"Ansom's ability doesn't track a target. It only hits where he specifies." He looked to Malik for confirmation and the man nodded.

"And Ansom's greatest talent has always been predicting his enemy's movements. I knew you were going to be beside me because you think too much. Because you know that I know better. Ansom thinks the same way."

Ellen's form began to waver again. "He's telling you to go with your instincts," she clarified before disappearing.

"So, it's not that he hates me. He's scared of me." Evander found himself grinning, replaying every instance that should have made it painfully obvious.

Malik gave him a small, bitter smile. "I'm fairly certain he still hates you, but that's more a fault of mine. That, and you caused him to fail. That is his greatest fear."

"A fault of yours?"

"When your brother was born, I was a very different man. I didn't change until much later, shortly before we had you."

Evander blinked at him. "Brother?"

"The clan children are raised communally. The head of the clan keeps records in an attempt to breed certain abilities, but there are several cases that a couple would have more than one child together." Malik examined him carefully. "Does this change your resolve?"

Evander thought about it for a moment. "No. He's power mad and clearly is not interested in any sort of blood tie. Besides, I was never one to put much stock in blood relations."

Malik smiled again. "Then you'll be fine. Ansom was scared of you because he cannot predict where you will be with your magic. He trained you into a very specific mindset that makes you predictable. If you lose that predictability, you will be fine."

Evander gave a nervous chuckle. "It sounds almost too simple."

"Sometimes that's just how it is."

# Chapter Ten
Month of the Maiden 17, 421 HE

Gentle music could be heard from the room where Caiden had once again taken the old king when breakfast was finished. Malik stood aside to let Evander enter and he found the pair huddled close together, their eyes glazed over, each with a hand on the tiny music box that was playing.

Evander found himself staring in wonder at the shelves upon shelves of music boxes. He'd never seen so many in one place before. It must have cost a fortune. Several.

"Where did all of these come from?" he asked, keeping himself quiet so he wouldn't disturb Caiden and his grandfather.

"I made them," Malik said quietly as he entered the room. He slowly began picking up the boxes that sat around the royal pair, cleaning them off and returning them to their proper places. Every shelf was labeled, most by year and date, but there were also larger boxes or chests with the names of other countries or people.

"Made them?"

"It would cost a fortune to keep buying them, so I made a few friends and I got the parts to make them in bulk. I can make a hundred small ones before I need to order more."

"That is amazing."

Malik strolled over to one of the shelves and started collecting boxes. "I wonder about that."

"How do you know what memories go where?" he asked, marveling at how easily the older man picked out the items he wanted.

Malik raised an eyebrow at him and held up the box in his hand. A date and name were carved into the side.

"He used to have them all jumbled in boxes before I told him to do that." Ellen's voice was a soft chuckle. He was adjusting to hearing her but not seeing her and he swore that he could almost feel the woman standing beside him, though she had no physical presence.

Malik set his burden down on one of the small tables. "The keys are in the boxes. Put them back when you're finished. If you touch any of the others, I will cut off your hands."

Evander was shocked by the venom in that statement, glancing over at Caiden and his grandfather who were still lost in another memory.

"He has earned the right to my memories and because it was his wish, I've allowed your Prince to handle them as well. But let me make this very clear. You are being given permission to look through these.

That is all. Anything else will be considered a trespass on par with the worst of crimes. Clear?"

Evander nodded mutely. He had never thought of it that way. Malik's talent was so useful that he had forgotten it was a look into the man's thoughts. His feelings, his senses, his physical sensations. It was a moment of the man's life that was being handled and looked at by people who had no business being in his mind in that way. He supposed there was no such thing as privacy with his ability.

He picked up the first of the music boxes with a newfound care and respect, carefully curling up in a chair before taking out the key and winding the instrument.

*A young boy stood in front of a group of targets, some only a few feet away, some farther back. Others hung from the ceiling or the walls around him.*

*"Begin."*

*As soon as the cue was given, the child started throwing. He had several knives in his off-hand, more strapped to his body, and an array of various items around him. In a matter of seconds, all had been launched. Rather than watching the knives hit their targets — as he knew they would — Malik watched the boy himself.*

*Ansom's eyes trained on a target, the knife left his hand, his eyes switched to the next. It was extraordinarily fast, but Malik could see the flaw in the child's ability very easily. Against a stationary target, he would not miss. However, it seemed that his ability only ensured that the projectile would hit a specific spot that was targeted in space, not the target itself.*

*That was the theory, at least.*

*The child grinned as all the targets were taken down and each had a blade directly in one of the kill spots. The gathered members were amazed. They congratulated Ansom, commending his amazing ability. Malik hummed. He'd have to point out the flaws before the praise got to his head.*

Evander replaced the key and closed the box. It was strange seeing Ansom as a child. He'd always been so severe and controlling throughout Evander's experience with him. He set the music box aside and picked up the next one.

*Malik watched the boy frown at the mechanism in front of him. A series of targets were attached to rope and pulleys.*

*"Umm, what is this?" he asked slowly, recognizing the test.*

*Malik nodded to another of the clan members who took up a spot by the pulleys. "A test," he answered.*

*"Test? But you've already tested me."*

*"Yes, but this is something new. Hit the targets."*

*Ansom took his stance and as soon as he gave the go ahead, the child threw.*

*And missed.*

*The targets had moved as the knife left the boy's hand.*

Malik observed Ansom as the child processed his first failure. His face flushed red with outrage.

"That's not—!"

"Try again," Malik ordered. He'd make the kid realize his limitations even if he had to force him to fail repeatedly. He'd spent too long being praised for his ability.

"But—!"

"Again," he snapped. This time, the targets kept moving in a steady rhythm. Ansom took his stance again and Malik could see the child struggling for the first time in his life.

He missed.

His ability was backfiring. In order to lock onto the point he needed to hit, his eyes had to be on it. Which meant he couldn't track the target and activate his ability or else it would be locked on several steps behind the moving target.

Ansom was becoming increasingly frustrated as he continued to fail. And Malik kept forcing him to do it again.

Finally, the boy threw down his knives, tears of frustration brimming in his eyes.

"Again," Malik's voice echoed in the almost empty training room.

"No! I can't!"

The blow was quick and harsh as Malik's hand lashed out to cuff the boy's head. Ansom recoiled, stumbling forward and staring up at him completely shocked. It was the first time he'd ever refused an order, *it was the first time he'd failed, so it was also the first time he'd been hit.*

*"I said to do it again," Malik growled at the child.*

*"But—"*

*"You can. You're just doing it wrong." If the arrogant brat would let go of his prior thinking and predict where the targets would be, then he wouldn't be having the problem. "Now get up and do it again. Correctly, this time."*

*There was a flash of anger in the boy's eyes as he slowly stood. Good. Maybe he'd improve if he thought of it as a challenge.*

Evander stared at the memory in his hand. That was not the Malik he'd met. He could feel the violence that he'd been capable of, but the man didn't give off the same feeling now. He shook his head and reached for the next one.

*"That is amazing," one of the younger members gaped at Ansom as the teenager finished his exercise.*

*Ansom gave a smug little grin, his eyes glancing over to Malik for a moment. "This much is nothing," he declared. "My ability makes it absurdly simple."*

*"What I wouldn't give to have an ability to track my target."*

*Malik ground his teeth. The boy had taken his advice to a whole new level of obsession. Malik had to replace the pulleys in the mobile training room from how much the child had practiced. Now any time he tried to intervene in the other's bragging, it only turned into another chance for Ansom to prove himself as the 'best'.*

*The worst of it was, every task the boy was given, he succeeded at. Every question had an answer and it was always correct, even if only by technicality. He never failed. It fed into his flaws while simultaneously making it seem like he didn't have any faults.*

*Ansom had been elected as the Prince's Guardian despite Malik's best efforts. No one seemed to realize just how ill-suited the brat was to the role. They only saw the glamor that was his ability. Sure, the teen was powerful, he was smart, he was quick to learn, discrete, strong, well-trained, and brilliant at strategy and tactics, but he was completely and utterly unsuited.*

*The backwards and convoluted thought made him growl. He needed to find a way to either knock him down a peg, or get rid of him entirely.*

A perfectionist, stubborn thinker, set in his ways, obsessed with appearances. Things that Evander suspected but now knew for certain. He immediately reached for the next memory.

*"I will not be stepping down," Malik declared.*

*There was muttering amongst the gathered clan members.*

*Ansom had the audacity to actually laugh. "Excuse me? Look, I know that you don't like me. It's fairly obvious. But now you're trying to hang on to your power just to... do what?"*

*"Ansom. If I give you this, it will spell the end of our hard work."*

*"Malik, I understand your jealousy. Truly. However, I am not about to defend myself to someone who clearly will say and do anything to keep the power to himself."*

*"What?"*

*"You heard me. Honestly, I never thought you'd stoop so low."*

*He was too late. It was clear. Too many had fallen to Ansom's way of thinking. No one would stand up to the man. And... no one would stand up for him. He didn't blame them, he'd been... unforgiving over the years and he'd made the changes too late. He couldn't stop this from happening.*

*Ansom smirked at him.*

*He couldn't do anything. Ansom had finally won. He should have known.*

--†--

Maiden, 18

"Eva."

Evander frowned, slowly stirring as Caiden shook his shoulder. He sat up, stretching and cracking his neck. He'd fallen asleep in the Music Room, surrounded by memories of Ansom, specifically Ansom's sparring practices, his fights, scenes that portrayed his way of thinking. His habits. He felt tired, as though he'd lived a few years more.

"Ready?" the prince asked.

"Did Malik already tell you?"

"What, that Ansom's ability is a sham? I already knew that. I just wasn't sure." He grinned at him.

"So, did you do anything else while I was occupied?" Evander asked.

"I think I know where to stage the ambush," Caiden replied, leaning his hip against the chair across from the servant.

"Oh?"

"There are some ruins where we used to camp. About twelve miles north-east of the capital. Plenty of shadows and I know it like the back of my hand already. If we can lead Ansom there, we'd have the advantage."

Evander hummed. He remembered the spot, but it had been so long since they'd gone outside the castle grounds on anything less than official business, he'd completely forgotten about it. "Sounds like you have this all figured out."

"Do you know how to beat him?" The prince raised his eyebrows, crossing his arms.

"I think so." Evander gave a slow nod.

"Then we've both done our parts. C'mon. Pretty sure Malik wants us gone as soon as possible. He might throw us out himself if we don't get a move on."

"What gave that away I wonder?"

Caiden jumped, spinning around as Malik leaned against the door frame. Evander chuckled.

"Go on, little prince. I'd like to have a word with your handler." The words were harsh, but the man's tone was friendly. Certainly coming from a man who cared nothing for Caiden's supposed authority. Caiden bristled but made his escape.

"I'll be downstairs then."

Malik watched him leave, then turned to Evander. "Think you're ready for this?"

"As ready as I can be." Evander shrugged.

Malik nodded, walking to one of the shelves that Evander had been forbidden to touch. He took a single box from its place and Evander knew immediately that it was something precious. It was larger, making room for a larger wheel, which meant a longer song and longer memory. It was also made from a dark wood, carved with vines, and sanded and stained where the others were simplistic in their design.

"When all is said and done, come back here. This will be waiting for you. Think of it as an incentive."

"Incentive?"

"To survive."

# Chapter Eleven
Month of the Maiden 22, 421 HE

Evander dropped down to where Caiden kept a fire going. "If he keeps going at this speed, we'll be seeing him tonight or tomorrow if he decides to attack during the day." he dusted off his hands, his fingers still a bit sore from climbing over the ruins in an attempt to spot Ansom's approach.

"Tonight, then? I doubt he'd come during the day, not to mention the cloud cover." Caiden gestured upwards.

They both looked up. The clouds were thick and heavy. There would be no shadows by moonlight tonight. They'd have to rely on the fire.

"How much fuel do we have?" Evander asked, looking back to the prince.

"Enough. We've spent the last few days gathering all we could."

"Throw it all in. Or as much of it as you can. We need the fire to last as long as possible."

Caiden hummed in reply, starting to build up the flames. They were both tense. Evander had been leading Ansom to their location slowly. Once he found the man, it was only a matter of leaving a few tracks then jumping and leaving a few more. He left a few every day, ensuring that they would have at least a little time.

Now he was almost there. They could only hope that they had enough of an advantage. Evander sighed, leaning against one of the crumbling walls. Thanks to Malik he now knew the assassin's fighting style, how he thought, his habits.

"Hey, Eva?" Caiden spoke up suddenly.

Evander hummed his acknowledgment as he examined the edge of his blade, bidding the other to continue.

"I know I kind of dropped the subject before… but can you tell me more about your training?"

"What do you want to know? I thought I already told you everything."

"Where did you go for that week, about… I don't know, I was eight. I remember I ran all over the castle searching for you, but everyone said you were away on the Vladimir clan's training camp."

Evander frowned, trying to remember the instance he was talking about. It was so rare for him to be separated from the prince that he honestly couldn't think of it. Then he remembered, and instantly wanted to forget again. Gooseflesh covered his arms and he shivered at the memory.

"It was a training camp. Just the last round of testing before they left me alone. For the most part. Everyone goes through it."

"Oh?" Caiden examined him. "What did they test you on?"

"Endurance," he answered, hoping that the man would drop it.

"Endurance…?"

No such luck. Evander sighed. "It's tailored to the trainee, so it's different every time."

"But what do you have to do? You say endurance, but couldn't you just run laps around the castle until you collapse?"

Evander let out a dark chuckle. "If only," he muttered.

"Eva, what the hell did they do?" Caiden was getting annoyed with his dodging.

"Pain, Caiden. You have to endure pain. Before anything happens, they give you a word, some random word. If you say this word at any point in the week, it stops. Whoever is watching you will pull you out or whoever is hitting you will stop. However, if you say it then you fail. The goal is to survive the week without saying it. You either reach the end and pass, give up and use the safe word, or you die."

He glared over at the prince who was staring at him wide-eyed.

"But—Eva, if I was eight, you were only ten! Are you kidding me? What do they do?"

"Well, it's not like I knew it was my testing period. I was called into the training room, didn't think much of it, then Ansom just grinned at me and told me to listen well. He said 'rutabaga' and the next thing I knew someone was behind me, covering my nose and mouth with some kind of drug-soaked cloth, then I woke up in the dark." He trailed off with a hum, then realized that Caiden was listening with rapt attention.

He sighed before continuing. "It was freezing. I woke up with a headache. I could barely see. It was damp. I could hear water somewhere relatively nearby. I had no idea what time it was. I had no idea what was going on. It took me a few minutes before I realized that I was being tested."

"What did you do? Where were you?"

"I was in one of the underwater caves by the coast. Farther north, though I didn't know that at the time. I got up and tried to feel my way around. It was freezing. My clothes were damp at that point and the walls were slimy with algae. I remember thinking that it was weird that there was algae on the walls even though I was above water. I felt around for a while but there was no way out. There were walls on three sides. One had a hole in the wall, but I didn't think I'd fit, and the other sloped down from what I could tell, but there was only water that way."

"Then…"

"Yeah. I realized after about a half hour that the water level was rising. That's when I figured out I was in one of the caves. The only exit was underwater, and I had no idea where to go once I dove or how long I'd have to be under for. Not to mention it was freezing."

"How'd you get out then?"

Evander smiled. "Well, after that, I sat there for a few minutes. And I watched the water level keep rising. Then realized that I could see the water and my surroundings fairly well for what was supposed to be an underwater cave. I looked up and saw that there was an opening farther up that I hadn't seen before, since the sun hadn't gotten there yet. I could see where the walls would reflect where it was wet, and it was only a half foot below the opening... maybe. I wasn't sure at the time, but I didn't want to risk drowning."

"So, what, you just waited?"

"Pretty much. I won't lie, it was terrifying. There came a point when I heard the sudden rush of water and the water level was going up really fast. I couldn't see any more, so I had to try and stay as still as I could while being pushed and pulled by the current. I actually missed the opening. Got stuck on the cave ceiling and went under for a minute." He shivered at the memory. "It was so cold I thought I might die of hypothermia before I drowned, but I managed to get over to the point below the opening and the water level kept going up. All I had to do was tread water until it wouldn't go up anymore. I just braced against the walls as well as I could and dragged myself out."

"So, where were you? Was there anyone there to help?"

Evander laughed. "No. I ripped off my clothes so they wouldn't sap anymore body heat. I was shaking so bad I could barely stand, it was dark out, in the early winter, and I had nothing to help me survive. I rolled around in the dirt and grass to try and dry off and get feeling back in my limbs. I managed to find some kindling and I pulled the laces from my shirt to help get a fire started."

"How the hell did you manage to survive that?"

"Honestly, I have no idea. I managed to get my clothes dry pretty quickly so it's not like I was naked for all that long, I also didn't let myself sleep. Foraged some food once the sun was up again and started making my way back to the castle. Took a few days, but I did it."

"A few days? Eva, you were gone for a week."

Evander shifted uncomfortably. "Yeah, once I got to the castle grounds, the one who must have been assigned to watch me revealed herself and told me to go through the Inner Castle. So, I did. I thought it was over."

"You were wrong?" Caiden guessed.

"Dead wrong." Evander sighed. "Got jumped almost as soon as I got to the training room and dragged to an area I'd never been to before."

This time it was Caiden shifting nervously. "What happened?"

"Oh, they beat me senseless. Using every tool in the arsenal. Every torture technique. All the while the administrator would be talking in the background 'all you have to do is say the word. All of it will end, I promise.' Her voice was so soothing… 'Just say it. That's all you have to do.'"

"And you didn't?"

Evander snorted out a laugh. "No. And I told her that too. 'If I do that, sure it'll stop. You'll just kill me, and I won't have to feel it anymore.' She didn't like that answer. She didn't like that I could speak at all."

"I thought you said that they'd stop if you said the safe-word."

"That's what they told us. But everyone who failed was never heard from again. We were told they ran away, that they were given alternate positions throughout the kingdom. It never sat well with me. I guessed, and I was right."

"So, you never said the safe-word?"

"Never."

"How long did they keep you there?"

"About... Hell if I know, it was a long time ago."

"Eva, you were ten. You're telling me that they tortured a ten-year-old for days?"

"I was ten. Riu was thirteen. Karen was nine. Another was fifteen." Evander shrugged. "We are assassins. We are spies. And we all know everyone else. If we were discovered and tortured for information, it wouldn't matter our ages."

"I guess... Still, it's barbaric."

"Necessary, but yes." He laughed. "I wouldn't go anywhere near the woman who'd administered my test for the next... well, actually I still avoid her if at all possible. She's nice. She actually apologized and always gives me little gifts when she sees me. She's fairly old now."

Caiden hummed but seemed content with the answers he was given.

"When we get home, I'm gonna ask Karen to make some mulled wine, the kind with apples and cinnamon that she made for my birthday. And pudding. And bread. Sweet bread and mulled wine." Caiden laughed, but it was a strained sound. "If she's still there, that is."

"She will be." Evander found himself reassuring him. "She's a tough woman, not to mention she got along well with Riu. I'm sure she'll be fine. There were several of them that didn't exactly follow Ansom's ideology but managed to keep their heads down enough to not be noticed. It'll be fine."

Caiden smiled but it was another voice that replied, a dark chuckle silencing the Prince before he could speak.

"Oh, really? You'll have to give me their names."

# Chapter Twelve
Month of the Maiden 22, 421 HE

Both of them turned towards the edge of the firelight. Ansom was skulking just out of view, his form nothing more than a darker patch of shade in the night.

"Now, Evander, I know we've had our misunderstandings, but I will offer you one last time. If you complete your duty, I won't be forced to kill you."

"You'd just kill me as soon as I went back with you." Evander drew out his daggers. "Besides, we both know you'll have just as hard a time with or without Caiden there." He poured a tone of mockery into his voice. Now that he knew Ansom's weakness, it was almost too easy to goad him.

The jab hit home and Evander sucked in a breath, fighting himself to hold perfectly still as the sound of a knife flying through the air made him want to duck. Had he done so, it would have killed him. As he stood, the weapon sailed past his side.

Evander darted forward, watched Ansom raise his weapons, and just before he came into striking distance, his foot struck a shadow and he dove, revealing the prince who'd been just behind him. He came out a few yards away, watching Caiden's blow strike against a dagger, deflected.

He drew one of the few throwing daggers he had left and threw, watching in annoyance as Ansom leaned back to avoid it. However, while the blade didn't hit, it allowed Caiden to get clear.

Ansom backed out of the light and for a second, Evander lost track of him.

"Eva!"

Evander pulled with his ability and twisted. The knife grazed past his shoulder but didn't break skin.

"Two against one and I will still kill you both without any effort." Ansom's voice was a sigh of disappointment.

"Says the man who brought seven people to kill the failure and the pitiful little prince and still failed," Evander spat.

"I did not fail. It was a test of their strength and they overestimated themselves." Ansom's voice was more of a hiss, the words forced through gritted teeth.

Evander turned to find the man crouched atop a crumbling wall. The glint of steel in the firelight, and Evander ran forward again, keeping the shadows constantly shifting and hiding his form. Ansom was so focused on trying to kill him that he seemed not to notice Caiden as the prince slowly made his way around the ruin to get behind him.

Evander danced, leaving just enough of himself exposed to keep Ansom's attention. Caiden was quick.

Just as he entered the man's peripheral vision he lunged, not giving the assassin any chance to perceive him.

It was almost inhuman how quickly Ansom moved, his body twisting with perfect balance on his perch, a hand catching the prince around the throat. He used Caiden's momentum to spin and throw the younger man into the ground.

Caiden hit hard and slid, crashing to a stop when he hit a pile of rubble.

"Caiden!" Evander twitched in the prince's direction, stopping short of getting his head bashed in by a rock. Ansom must have been running out of knives.

"You should know better than to take your eyes off of me, Evander."

Evander turned to face him as he stood atop the wall and glared.

"Now, now, what's that look for? The meek little servant is nowhere to be found. How unfortunate." The older assassin jumped and rolled to break his fall; the movement made with an effortless grace.

Evander didn't let him recover. He sprinted forward and forced himself not to think. Not to trust the training that had been hammered into his head until he was fighting instinct itself. Ansom raised his arm and threw. Evander didn't deviate his path, he didn't try to dodge, and the dagger sailed past his left side. As soon as Ansom realized he wasn't dodging left, he threw another and once again Evander forced himself not to dodge. This one skated past his right side.

Ansom snarled and threw straight at him and Evander dove forward. The dagger went above his head as he pulled himself through a shadow, appearing a few feet to Ansom's right. He threw a dagger at him to keep his attention and watched the man smack it aside. By then, Evander was close enough to engage in melee combat.

If he could just keep Ansom up close, then he couldn't use his ability. Instead of locking blades, Ansom dropped his and grabbed Evander as he got within range. They stood in a deadlock for a moment.

As long as Ansom had a hold of him, he couldn't use his ability either.

Granted, he could attempt to pull him into the shadows and let him suffocate, but Evander wasn't entirely sure that he'd be able to stop halfway through. He'd tried it after the fight with the elites and it was an instant teleportation, he couldn't just stop. That and even if he succeeded, Ansom wouldn't let go once they were in there and then they'd both end up dead.

*Well, maybe as a last resort.*

For a man in his forties, Ansom was just as strong as someone in their prime. Experience made up for any physical loss. Evander took a deep breath. While his instinct was to try and hook his leg around Ansom's feet to try and trip him, he struggled against the urge and instead shifted his weight and waited until Ansom took advantage of the movement to try and overpower him.

He was prepared for it and used that power against him. He flipped them, pushing Ansom into the ground then giving a yelp as he was kicked. Ansom had managed to get his feet between them and used the position to launch him over his head.

Evander rolled, saw Ansom in the process of throwing, and dove into the next shadow he hit. He came out only a pace away, swinging at the man, pleased when his blade skated across his back. The wound was too shallow to kill, the slash going through leather armor, catching spine and rib. It didn't have enough power to get past the bone to a kill point, but he knew it would hurt. Evander landed in Ansom's shadow and dove into it. He popped up some ways away and saw Ansom's expression of fury.

He danced. He was a rush of motion, diving into and out of shadows, randomizing his entrances, sometimes nowhere near his target, others he came out with blades spinning. Evander was a constant barrage of movement. Ansom fell into a rhythm with him. He was adjusting to the pattern, or the lack thereof.

Then finally, Ansom hit. Evander knew where his mistake was, he'd tried for one too many passes. It wasn't a deep cut, just across his chest since he'd managed to stop his forward momentum in time. He threw himself away before the other could follow up with another blow.

To his surprise, Ansom stood, daggers at the ready a few yards away instead of following after him.

The elder assassin smirked at him with a predatory glee that made him cautiously take stock of his surroundings. Then Evander realized with a growing sense of dread that his back was up against the fire now.

He would have to step forward to enter any shadows, and that motion was much more obvious. Ansom would kill him the second he moved.

He could pull his shadows and try to disorient his opponent while he moved into a better position, but he'd given that trick away while trying to distract him for Caiden. He was stuck unless he was willing to roll through fire to try and get away.

That would put him at an even worse disadvantage. His gaze slid to Caiden, who was struggling into a standing position, but he was clearly hurt. He winced in pain as a blade shot past his head, barely grazing his neck.

Ansom tisked. "A shame. You were doing so well, too." He studiously dusted himself off and slid a familiar knife from its sheath at his thigh.

Evander's throwing knife that he'd left behind when escaping with Caiden.

"With this, it'll be almost too easy. Poor prince. His own servant killed him in cold blood, I was simply too late to save him." His voice was pitched into an annoying, honey coated sympathy. "Don't worry. You won't have to witness it."

He flipped the dagger in his hand, pulled back his arm, and he threw. Evander didn't move, he couldn't. Caiden moved faster than Evander ever thought possible. He'd been in motion as Ansom had started talking but suddenly he was in front of him, arms outstretched.

Evander saw it: his own shadow thrown against Caiden's back. He didn't have time to wonder if it would work, it had to. He lunged forward, dragging himself through the shadow, through Caiden, sword first.

A choked noise and resistance against his blade made him look up. Ansom's face was turned to the left, his knife embedded in the shadow that was splintered off to the side. The assassin's expression was one of shock, disbelief, and no small amount of anger.

"You guessed wrong," Evander muttered, driving the sword home as he rose from Ansom's shadow.

It was an odd feeling as the man shuddered, his breath leaving him as he went limp. Evander had killed before. After all, there had been several attempts on Caiden's life in the past. Yet this one felt hollow, unreal.

Ansom was dead.

Evander looked up at Caiden then froze, his heart dropping into his stomach. Caiden was on the ground, Ansom's—his dagger, deep in his stomach. He felt like he couldn't breathe.

"Caiden?" He ran forward in a panic, afraid to touch him lest he make it worse. "Caiden!"

"Quit... yelling." The man's voice was wet sounding, his breath wheezing.

Relief broke over him. "Caiden, you have to stay awake. I don't know how to fix this."

A weak chuckle. "You can't..."

"Shut up, there has to be something."

Caiden huffed out a laugh, his hand pressed to the wound, the knife still in him, giving him a little more time before he bled out. "Eva... you don't even know the difference... between an herb and a weed..."

"I know, dammit! Just... shit." His throat was tight, his eyes burning as he tried desperately to think of something, anything.

"It's okay."

"No, it's not. Just... Gods, just please, please tell me what to do."

The prince just smiled at him, his eyes glassy, face quickly becoming white.

"Why did you do that if you knew he was aiming to kill?"

"Because... he needed to die... and you wouldn't let the chance... go to waste." Talking seemed to take effort for him.

"Idiot. I hated you... for so damn long." His voice broke. "Why..."

Caiden chuckled but it came out as a wheeze, his limbs starting to tremble. "You never hated me. Just jealous, right?"

Evander stared at him. He felt like his soul was slowly being shredded as he gently took hold of the man's hand, keeping pressure on the wound since Caiden couldn't.

He knew. He'd always known. He'd never truly hated Caiden. How could he? The prince spent his days lazing about, playing, having fun, yet he commanded all the respect, all of the love and adoration without having to do anything. He'd hated him for that. He'd worked so hard for so long, only to be abused, cursed, and spat upon for no reason over and over again. He'd hated it.

He gave the prince a miserable smile. "That obvious?"

"You never had it in you... to hate." Caiden paused, closing his eyes as he gasped for breath. "I figured it out... a while ago."

Evander squeezed the cool fingers in his hand. The prince's grasp was quickly weakening.

"I'm glad really... As much as I loved our days in the castle.... This last month... was definitely... the best..." Caiden's words were soft, the last leaving his lips on a sigh.

"I... yeah. It was fun." Evander slowly forced out the reply as Caiden's trembling finally ceased. "Caiden?"

Caiden didn't reply.

"Caiden?" He gently shook his shoulder.

Nothing.

"Eva!"

He didn't have the willpower to raise his head at the call. It was only when Riu was grabbing him and dragging him away that he seemed to wake up. He tried to shrug her off, only for her to yank him back while Karen knelt beside Caiden.

"Karen?" he asked slowly.

"I received a message from Malik. I brought her along, fearing the worst." Riu's hands were a comforting weight, her presence warm against his back as they waited for Karen to finish.

The cook sat back, looking over her shoulder at them. "He's already gone into shock. He isn't dead yet, but he is dying."

"But there has to be something. Anything!" Evander could feel himself shaking, trying desperately to keep his panic in check. Karen gave Riu a skeptical look. Evander turned towards the girl. "Riu, please, please tell me. Anything. I don't care what it is, there has to be a way."

She chewed on her lower lip. "My ability swaps souls. If we put an injured soul in a healthy body, it might encourage him to wake up. If we put a healthy soul in an injured body, they wouldn't die."

Evander stared at her, hope a cruel flame in his chest. "Will it work?"

"I don't know. It may just kill both—"

"Riu, if you switch mine and Caiden's souls, would it work?"

She made a noise in the back of her throat, a myriad of conflicting emotions flickering over her features. "Maybe?"

"Do it. Please, Riu, you have to do it."

"You might both end up dead."

"So?"

She hugged him, her arms tightening around him briefly. "You may not value your life, but I do. And I know you aren't going to listen to me." Her forehead bumped against his. "Fine."

He let her direct him, his body mirroring Caiden's as he laid down.

"You're sure?" she asked as she settled above his head.

He looked up at her. "Riu. It's not that I don't value my life. It's just worth very, very little if I don't have anything to do with it." He was a miserable wreck and he knew she saw that. He didn't know how to live outside of taking care of stupid, irresponsible princes.

She sighed and placed her hand, cupping the back of his head with her fingertips pressed into the base of his skull. She did the same to Caiden before leaning down and pressing her lips against his temple.

"I promise I'll bring him back to you."

"You better." He let his eyes close as a wave of dizziness made his vision fade, his body slowly going numb.

# Chapter Thirteen
Month of the Maiden 26, 421 HE

Evander blinked. His body felt cumbersome and sore. He had an odd feeling of disconnection, like there was a delay between his mind and body. He slowly turned his head, finding himself in the familiar surroundings of Caiden's room.

*Why am I in Caiden's bed?* It wasn't beyond the prince to insist that his servant sleep in the larger, more comfortable bed when he was hurt, but he couldn't remember getting injured to that extent.

A loud meow preceded Mira butting her head against his cheek. She was excited to see him and she rubbed against him, mewling the whole while. It made him chuckle, raising a hand to try and pet her. He didn't have the coordination to do much more than hug her to him. The cat seemed to enjoy this for all of five seconds before squirming out of his arms and running off.

Evander slowly levered himself into a sitting position. Something didn't feel right. His movements were clumsy at best. It took him a few tries before he managed to get the blanket off of him. Then he swung his legs over the edge of the bed and pushed himself to his feet.

He swayed a moment, disoriented as his line of sight was a few inches higher than what he was used to. He tried to step forward, but his legs felt too heavy. He couldn't quite get them to move as he wanted. He stumbled, his knees refusing to hold his weight and depositing him on the floor with a loud thump and clatter as he tried to catch himself, but only succeeded in knocking a silver platter off its perch.

He stared at it, his reflection only slightly distorted in the tray. Red hair, a pale freckled face, blue eyes wide and confused. He tilted his head and the reflection moved as well. He was staring at Caiden but…

The door crashed open as Sir Hayden rushed into the room followed closely by Jedidiah and the Court Priest.

"Your Highness!" The physician directed Sir Hayden to pick him up and put him back in bed.

Evander looked around for a moment, disoriented, before realizing that they were talking to him. The knight was already in the process of lifting him, and Evander saw the scar that stretched across the side of his face. Then he wondered why Hayden was the first response, not Sir Michael.

"Sir Michael…" His words were slurred, his tongue felt heavy, as though he couldn't convince it to form the words the way he wanted.

"Your Highness, please lay down. We will explain that in a moment." Jedidiah pulled the blankets over him and beckoned the priest forward.

Maddox was younger, having recently taken the position from the previous pastor when the other retired. Evander had been warned about him, they all had. He was one of the few ability users allowed to use his power publicly. The Exorcist, they called him. Able to see the soul of a person, able to see their ability if they were an ability user, able to nullify it. It was a horrifying ability, disgustingly unfair.

That was until he met the man. He'd had to. When the priest was introduced to Caiden, he wouldn't stop staring at him and Evander remembered how terrified he'd been. He was so sure he was going to be outed and killed. Yet, the pastor simply introduced himself and said, "You have a strong soul."

The compliment had caught him off guard, but it quickly became apparent that the priest wasn't going to tell on any of them unless they were a threat. Now, he wasn't so sure if they remained in his good graces. After all, most of them would be branded as traitors now.

Maddox was already frowning as he stepped forward, examining him.

"Well?" Sir Hayden demanded.

Evander stared at the priest and the man stared back. He knew. He had to know.

"He seems free of any and all magical influence. He is… himself."

Evander stared at him and received a pointed glare in return.

"Oh, thank the Gods. Your Highness, we feared you'd never wake." Jedidiah gave a sigh of relief.

"What... happened?"

"Evander assassinated the King, Queen, and the young princess, then went after you. However..."

Sir Hayden shared a look with Jedidiah. "I saw you both falling from the castle window. You just disappeared."

"Then Ansom took the throne. We thought that something was wrong. We tried to find you before he did, but we were too late. We found the bodies of several members of the Vladimir clan. We followed Ansom's trail, but we must have been a day or two behind him."

"And... Evander?" he hesitated before using his own name to refer to the prince.

"Evander was gone. Ansom was already dead when we found you. I didn't believe Ansom's tale, but was it true?"

"I..." he paused, trying to mimic Caiden's way of talking. "No. He saved me from Ansom. We were hiding when they found us again. We managed to defeat most of his elites, but we ran from him." The words came easier, his mouth forming the sounds easily as he spoke as Caiden would. The less he thought about it, the easier it became. "We trapped him and... I-I guess I was injured." he subconsciously touched the thick scar on his stomach, those final moments still replaying in his mind.

"So, he was responsible for it. That bastard," Jedidiah growled. "Beg your pardon, Your Highness."

The older man bowed and quickly gave him a check over, determining him weak but healthy.

Sir Hayden was watching him with an odd look.

"Um, how long have I been sleeping?"

"Only four days. You must be hungry. We'll have the servants bring something. Maddox, since you're the highest rank here, please inform his Highness of anything else. I must begin preparations." Sir Hayden bowed and left the room.

There was a heavy silence that followed. Evander glanced nervously between the priest and the Physician, both of whom were staring at him.

"Uh…" he began to speak, struggling to think of what Caiden would do in this situation.

"Riu actually got it to work, didn't she?" Jedidiah asked quietly.

Evander felt himself pale. "How did…?"

"You have distinctive mannerisms, I could tell by the way you guarded yourself, you weren't Caiden. That and this." The old physician chuckled and held up the small golden earring, the ruby glinting in the sunlight. Then the old man sobered. "Where is he?"

"I don't know. Riu must have taken him." Evander held out his hand and the Physician placed the treasure in his palm. The pieces were sealed by magic. They would only come off if the wearer died. Evander turned the piece over in his hand. Had it come off when they switched bodies? Had it been when Caiden had stopped breathing? Had Caiden died?

Was Caiden dead? He wouldn't put it past Riu to put him in Caiden's body and leave him to rule in the prince's stead. It would avoid an inevitable war over the throne. But why wouldn't they tell him? Where did they go? He supposed that they couldn't come back to the castle, not with 'Evander' still being wanted and the entire Vladimir clan being branded as criminals.

His head was still trying to catch up to the events.

The priest sighed and ran his hand through his hair, bringing Evander back to the present. "Look, we need to hold the coronation ceremony soon. In about a month at the latest. The crown is a magical artifact. It's tied to the royal bloodline and shines with the 'Divine Light' when a new king is crowned as proof of their claim. It's one of the reasons why the Royal family has remained on the throne for so many years."

Evander stared at him. "But is it blood or soul related?"

"Both."

Evander leaned back. "So…"

"We can fake it. You're in Caiden's body, there's the blood, but magic deals mostly in the soul, so while it would trigger the first part of the spell, it won't finish it. I can try and cause the same effect. In the meantime, do you know the prince's speech to the people?"

"I wrote half of it."

"Evander."

Evander looked up at the priest as the man began to move towards the door.

"You are Caiden now. Don't mess it up." He pulled open the door then looked back at him once more.

"Oh, and the remaining members of the Vladimir clan have all been imprisoned, awaiting your sentence."

Evander felt his blood run cold.

--†--

## Dragon 20

*Evander laid still as the child crawled into his bed, the young prince's body quivering as he cried. He ignored him, pretending to sleep.*

*"I'll fix it," the child sniffled. "I'll make it so magic isn't bad anymore."*

Evander swallowed hard. His heart was pounding against his ribs, his hands trembled, and he felt ill. He sat upon the plain wooden chair that had been brought out for the event, placed at the base of the dais where the thrones sat.

It was still a week before his coronation, but this had been put off for too long and he'd received so many questions and complaints that he had to call for the Vladimir clan to be brought forward.

There had been over sixty of them before the coup. Ten men and women knelt in front of him. Many were injured, clearly abused during their time in the dungeons. All were resigned to their fates.

Their charges were read and then silence befell the room. There was a gallery of people who'd gathered to watch the judgment, the council members who would advise the decision, and the gathering of nobles who'd been invited to view the procedure. Evander had accompanied Caiden to these hearings for years and had been present when Caiden was finally told to do it himself.

"Your Highness, with your permission, we would also like to bring the priest here," one of the Council members voiced. He was a small, wrinkled man, the one in charge of handling the treasury.

Evander nodded his consent.

Maddox was brought in and Evander could see the confusion on the man's face, which quickly gave way to outrage as he was practically shoved into the group of prisoners.

"What do you think you're doing?" Evander demanded before the priest could speak.

"He is a magic user as well. His ability allows him to see the ability of others. This would suggest that he was a part of this conspiracy as well, seeing as he has never accused any of the Vladimir clan of being magic users."

Evander took a deep breath and let it out slowly, sitting up straight. "Your fear of magic invites misunderstanding and shows a severe lack of information on the subject."

"Excuse me, Your Highness, but with all due respect—"

Evander raised a hand and the man fell silent. "I have studied it, extensively, as any of the nobility can attest to." He gestured towards the gathered nobles, several of whom bowed their heads in acknowledgment. Caiden had spent several years soaking up information on magic and magic users until Evander finally managed to curb his interests.

"From my understanding," he continued, "an ability must be activated or triggered in order to work. Unless Pastor Maddox walked around all day and night with his ability in use, there is no way that you can say that he knew of any of their magics. It is also shown through several studies that the use of abilities results in a drain of their energy. It would be exhausting to do such a thing. Therefore, it is clear that he'd only use it when asked to. He has served us diligently through the years and has always used his ability for our benefit."

He eyed the Council and was pleased to see them squirm. They had been taking liberties, claiming that he was still too ill, too weak, to properly give commands. They were trying to turn Caiden into a puppet and Evander would sooner die than allow that to happen. It had resulted in a rather stressful month.

"Pastor Maddox, please stand. I apologize for your treatment."

The man shoved away the guard and bowed deeply towards him. "My thanks, Your Highness."

"The charge against the Vladimir clan still stands, Your Highness. Their charge is treason and murder atop the charge of their having magic."

"You." Evander pointed at one of the younger clan members who looked up at him with fear. "You are Lawrence, correct?"

"Y-yes, Your Highness."

"Where were you the night of the coup?"

"I was in the servants' quarters."

"Yes, I recognize you. You were in one of the groups I arranged to escape the castle. Did you know of Ansom's plans?"

"No, Your Highness."

"Lies," one of the council members spat. The boy recoiled.

Evander ignored them, quickly thinking through what he was about to attempt. "What is your recount of the event?"

The boy blinked at him as though he hadn't expected the question. Evander listened as he slowly worked through the events of that night.

He'd been assigned to Sir Hayden's group and they were ambushed at the end of the passageway that they'd used to escape. Two of the assassins had tried to kill them all. Sir Hayden had been injured and Lawrence had used his ability to protect him and the others until the soldiers were able to defeat the assassins.

"Bring me Sir Hayden," Evander called, knowing that the knight would be nearby. He waited until the man was standing before him and asked him to recount his version of the events. After listening to all accounts that were able to be given, he concluded that everyone's version of the night matched. Including another two of the clan members whose stories were also supported.

"In light of this development, I withdraw the charges of treason and murder from these three," he declared.

"That does not excuse their use of magic," one of the council members pointed out.

"I am aware," he replied before moving on to the next person. They were all low-ranking members. Evander could clearly see that they didn't belong to either faction in their group. Those who followed Ansom had been killed during the coup or had fled once Ansom fell. Those who had been against the man had escaped with Riu during the chaos.

One by one, he listened to their stories. Most were revealed when they used their abilities to help their friends or to fight against Ansom's assassins. Then he came to one that he remembered quite clearly.

Melanie Vladimir was a maid in the castle. She had become the Queen's handmaiden when she married into the Kallenport Royalty. In other words, she was the Queen's assassin. Her ability: Midnight Murder. Anything she touched while her ability was active would lose its life force. It was slow working, only functioned at night, and left her victims as a distinctive husk. She told her tale with tearful conviction.

"What is your ability?" he asked.

"Excuse me?" she hesitated.

"Your ability, what is it?"

"J-just something simple. I can mend clothing."

Evander hummed and stood from his seat, casually approaching the girl much to the guards' disapproval. Once he stood in front of her, he drew out the dagger he wore on his belt. There was a flash of paranoia in the woman's face, blatant fear and disbelief, before he stabbed the blade into the hem of his shirt and wrenched it through the fabric with a loud tearing sound.

"Repair this," he commanded, easily stepping into her range and waving the guards off.

He watched her eyes flick around the room. Taking in the guards, their weapons, the crowd, the exits, and finally her eyes drifted to the dagger in his hand. He felt a small, scheming smile draw across his lips. Her eyes twitched to his own and he held her gaze, let his intent, his *knowledge* show through.

He watched the woman's spark of defiance sputter and die out into despair.

"I can't." Her voice was a faint whisper.

"What was that?" he asked, though he could hear her perfectly.

"I can't!" She slammed her fist into the ground, her head bowed, body quivering with the knowledge that she was now trapped.

Evander hummed and went back to his chair. "Melanie Vladimir. You stand on the charge of murder and treason. How do you plead?"

She glared, her lips curling into a snarl: every bit the assassin he knew. "I should have killed you myself."

"I have a proposition for you. Your crimes warrant hanging." He paused, letting the weight of her position settle. "However, if you confess. If you take an oath of truth and provide a full account of the events leading up to the coup including everyone involved. I will stay your execution."

She ground her teeth, glared around the room then finally settled her gaze on him. "Full immunity."

"I will not kill you," he countered, knowing she hadn't actually expected immunity but rather was attempting to haggle her sentence and treatment.

"No torture?"

"Not unless it is necessary. Which, given the notions of this deal, is doubtful."

"I will be given comforts?"

"You will receive items and such upon giving relevant information."

"After which I will be released."

"After which you will be called forward for retrial where it will be decided."

"Fine."

Evander let out a slight sigh of relief, inaudible to most though he could tell a few of the clan members saw it. By the end of the interrogations, he had managed to pardon all other members from the charges of murder and treason.

"Councilmen, allow me to ask a question." Evander's tone clearly said he didn't actually care for their permission.

"Of course, Your Highness." their speaker replied.

"Why is magic illegal?"

"It was after magic was used to try and overthrow your ancestors over a hundred years ago. It was for the safety of the kingdom." the speaker sounded concerned, clearly he either knew where he was heading with this line of questioning or he suspected the prince to be an idiot.

"Yet magic that is beneficial to us is allowed? For example, Pastor Maddox's?"

"Yes."

"So, a magic user who controls fire?"

"Will be executed." the councilman responded instantaneously.

"What if they use it to light candles? Or make sure a fire does not spread in a burning building?"

"E-excuse me?" there was some muttering from the other council members.

"There are many benefits to having a person who can control an element. Or in having someone who can shield their allies. And, might I add, there would be quite a use for an ability to manipulate fabric. They could make uniforms at a mere fraction of the usual costs." Evander spoke with quick, determined authority, making sure they couldn't interrupt though the speaker tried.

"W-well, you have a point, Your Highness, however, traditionally—"

"Our laws are there to protect the people. Any citizen who breaks these laws will be subject to punishment, correct? So, what is the point in having a law forbidding something so potentially beneficial?" Evander let his voice drop to a deeper, more commanding tone as he cut off the speaker.

"Your Highness, are you suggesting…?"

"I would like to abolish the law forbidding the use of magic in the kingdom of Kallenport." There was a great clash of noise from everyone around him.

"Order! Order!" One of the council members stood and pounded his fist against the table. "Your Highness, with all due respect, in order to do such a thing, you must have the Council's approval or you must be crowned King. Your coronation has yet to happen, so you must abide by our ruling on this matter." they had clearly abandoned using the speaker as their middleman, the head of the council taking over.

"And your ruling is?"

"Absolutely not, Your Highness. It poses too great a risk to the people."

"Is that so?" Evander stared the man down, clearly giving him a chance to back off.

"Yes." Clearly the old fool didn't get the hint. Usually they were so careful not to directly oppose him, especially in something where he was so clearly invested. They'd sabotage his efforts, delay the decrees, and all around be a pain in his ass, but they were growing bold to stand directly against him.

"Fine then. I will be putting off their judgment until after the coronation." He rose from his seat.

"Your Highness!" The Council were all shouting their disapproval until he turned his gaze unto them.

"Did you say something, Councilmen? I believe I said I was holding off their judgement. Unless you would rather yours be held instead?"

"We beg your pardon?" the speaker seemed to get annoyed with being spoken over despite his position and used the sudden silence of his peers to retake control.

"You all were present throughout the coup and all agreed to allow Ansom as regent despite the evidence against him. Why is that, I wonder?" Evander glared at them for a moment before walking towards the doors. "You are all dismissed. Guards, escort the prisoners back to their cells, cease all interrogations, and ensure their comfort."

He let out the breath he'd been holding as the doors closed behind him. He could only hope it would work. The Council was quickly forcing his hand. He hadn't really considered which of them was the traitor who conspired with Ansom, but he supposed it wouldn't hurt to just replace all of them.

He shook his head and started walking. No, he couldn't do that. They had too much experience to just be thrown away.

His control of Caiden's body was good enough now that there was very little delay between his intentions and his actions. He flexed his fingers and only then realized that he was still holding his dagger. He sheathed the weapon, nearing the end of the hall.

"Your Highness?"

He turned to see the Secretary's retainer trying to catch up to him. He was a young man with callused, ink stained fingers.

*Interesting.* Evander observed the man as he drew closer. He was light on his feet, not out of breath in the slightest as he came to a stop in front of him.

"Yes?" he asked, pausing.

"Do you truly intend to legalize magic?" the man asked.

"I do. It was a law that was passed in paranoia. It has no real place in our codes. Honestly, it does more harm than good."

"I see. Then I apologize, Your Highness."

Evander saw the flash of metal and instinctively pulled at the shadows around him. Only to find that they were completely unresponsive to his call. He dodged, taking a quick step backwards.

The man looked shocked, but he sank into a battle-ready stance. Evander looked past him, down the empty corridor, and strained his ears to listen for anyone coming from behind him. Finding no one, he let himself relax.

The would-be assassin frowned, clearly put off by his sudden change in demeanor. He wondered if he would be better off leaving the man alive for questioning.

The assassin slashed at him and Evander switched tactics stepping to the side, disappearing into the shadow on the wall. He appeared behind the man and without fanfare, grabbed him by the head and slammed him into the stone.

*Well, at least my ability hasn't abandoned me completely.* He examined his hands as though he could see the magic.

"Your Highness!" Sir Hayden ran towards him, his steps slowing down as he saw the man at his feet. The knight must have noticed the missing secretary and came to find him.

Evander stepped away from the body. "Apologies, Sir Hayden."

"Are you alright, Your Highness?" the knight asked, eyeing the assassin.

"I'm fine, though it would seem there's yet another conspiracy."

Sir Hayden turned his gaze to him and Evander found himself being scrutinized. "What shall I do, Your Highness?"

Evander tilted his head. "Have a few men keep an eye on the Council members. Do not report this." He gestured to the body. "One of them will slip up. Once you find one, it is only a matter of time before you can root out the others."

Hayden stared at him a moment longer before giving him a bow. "As you wish, Your Highness."

"As for the body, I'll leave it to you." He had barely finished the sentence before Hayden had stooped down to grab the man and promptly dropped him out the window.

"Now, I believe I have an incident report to burn, if you'll excuse me, Your Highness." The knight bowed again before heading down the hall.

Evander found himself grinning. The man may prove to be a problem eventually, but Caiden had always been fond of him and now, Evander could see why.

"There you are, Your Highness. Please come this way for your fitting." A servant found him as he turned the corner.

# Chapter Fourteen
Month of the Dragon 27, 421 HE

"Your Highness, it is nearly time."

The call was muffled through the door and Evander blew out a shaky breath. He hadn't been able to eat, his stomach flipping and turning itself into knots. He felt vaguely ill. He chuckled at himself, looking up at the mirror.

Caiden's face was still pale, the dark red of his hair brushing against his brow. He was still not used to seeing the Prince's face when he looked at his reflection. He dipped his fingers into the small tin of oil, slicking back the unruly strands so his face was clearly visible.

He would have been so pleased with himself, making Caiden look so regal. Then again, Caiden never would have sat still long enough for him to accomplish this. His clothing was well-made: a high-quality black tunic embroidered with silver thread, comfortable, and simple in design. It was matched with a deep, burgundy colored undershirt that was largely hidden, but it was the same color as the long, thin cape that was pinned at his shoulder. It was a gauzy fabric that would flow behind him as he walked.

He'd had to stand still, parade about, get pricked and poked and measured and prodded, manhandled as the tailor did his work for the better part of a week. He would have loved to see Caiden in it. Caiden would have loved it. He was never one for parties, for sitting and playing nice, but he'd always enjoyed dressing up for them. He'd once said that he felt like a different person, that he could just pretend that he was in costume and playing a role. Evander hadn't corrected him. He hadn't cared so long as the prince didn't embarrass himself.

"Your Highness?" His door slowly creaked open, a retainer poking his head in nervously. "Would you like any help with the preparations, Your Highness?"

"No. I've finished." He rose from his seat and turned, the boy quickly moving aside.

There was a small group of people waiting for him outside his door. All were younger servants, one of whom held a sheaf of parchment. The teenager shuffled through the papers, stuttering a list of instructions from Maddox. Evander was only half listening to the briefing as they walked.

The castle was quiet. Everyone was outside, waiting. It was a simple procedure. By now, the nobility, the ambassadors, and the visiting royalty would have all taken their seats. He heard the trumpets blare to announce the beginning of his journey to where he would be crowned.

The prince walks alone from the castle doors, only accompanied by his ever-loyal servant, the symbolic representation of the original pair that had built the kingdom, their trials and struggles, until arriving at the other end of the city where the last battle for the kingdom had taken place. Where King Kailyn himself was crowned by his brother Vladimir, witnessed and recognized by the other monarchs of the time.

The castle doors opened to a small fanfare and the kingdom's anthem could be heard as the citizens all were cued to sing. It was a disconcerting feeling, eerie. He stepped out onto the path, head held high, and he walked.

He would have walked just behind Caiden on his journey. The Council had been adamant that he find someone to replace him: for tradition's sake. Evander had refused. It was perhaps selfish, but he knew Caiden would have done the same. It was a time meant to honor their bond. The bond that had been fake, a cruel lie, twisted and bastardized for so many years.

It wasn't a long walk, the chill of autumn making it pleasant, the sound of hundreds of people singing the anthem over and over again to the point where Evander only heard it as noise. Caiden would have been jittery with excitement, despite his trepidation. He could see the grass, the hill that overlooked the city where pavilions had been set up along with chairs, daisies, and at the very crest, a throne.

The attending monarchs remained seated, as was their right, while all others stood upon his arrival. Maddox stood beside the throne and he stepped down as Evander approached.

To be crowned by another monarch or noble would show him to be subservient to them, so the priest had volunteered to become a neutral party and perform the ceremony instead.

Maddox had already undergone his pledge to denounce his relation to any and all other powers for this ceremony. Evander turned to face the assembled crowd and knelt.

Maddox began to speak, reading from a script. Evander was sure that he was replying, as he had practice, recited, and read. It had been hammered into his head because it was supposed to have been him reading that script for Caiden. It made his heart twist painfully at the thought. He wished that Malik were here, using his ability so that he could show it to the prince when he returned. If he returned.

"Please raise your head." Maddox's voice brought him out of his thoughts and he realized that the priest had already recited his vows and moved behind him.

The moment of truth then. He had already thought of any escape, any excuse he could make if the priest couldn't fake the Identification spell. There was none. Not a single path that he could use to get out. His heart was pounding so hard it was a wonder that no one heard it.

Evander lifted his head and held his breath as the priest gently slid the crown into place. A warm, tingling sensation swept through him for a moment before a burst of beautiful golden-white light swept over the assembled people. He rose to his feet, barely registering Maddox stumbling back.

He watched the nobles bow and cry at the sight of the 'Divine Light,' he could hear the citizens' cries rising up from the city and from the area around the hill. He took a breath and began to speak. He was too relieved, too shaken to truly remember the inspirational words that he'd helped Caiden memorize so long ago.

He turned and ascended to the throne, taking his seat and letting his voice ring out over the gathering, announcing the start of the festivities.

--†--

"Your Majesty." Evander turned to look at the King of Terravinter, escorting his second daughter Eudora.

"Your Majesty," he responded in kind.

"Congratulations on your coronation. It was magnificent. Your father, no doubt, would have been proud."

"Thank you."

"May I present my daughter, Princess Eudora. I believe you have not formally met. That awful occurrence delayed your meeting."

Evander watched as the girl swept a graceful curtsey, her eyes respectfully downcast. "A pleasure to meet you, Your Majesty."

Her voice was soft and sweet, her pale skin of a honeyed hue, her long dark hair swept up in an artful, yet simplistic style. She struck him as a mindless doll. Her movements were smooth and practiced, her words carefully annunciated. She seemed articulate for a fourteen-year-old but was following the steps set before her by others.

He dipped his head in greeting. "The pleasure is mine, Your Highness. I must say I am rather glad you were delayed. It would have been disastrous had you been present during the coup."

"I can take care of myself, Your Majesty." Her gaze flicked up to meet his own and he saw a spark of life in her that was quickly hidden away as her father's grip tightened on her arm.

"I beg your pardon, Sir. She is not yet used to social functions."

"It is quite all right. It was a rather traumatizing event, I'm sure. I apologize for reminding you of it." The girl muttered something under her breath that he couldn't catch. He resisted the urge to laugh. His first impression of the girl was quickly changing.

"On that note, what is your official statement on the event? We only heard what was told to us by our ambassadors." The king watched him with carefully contained suspicion.

*And your spies, I'm sure.* "My father's advisor betrayed him. Mine almost lost his life to save me."

"And where is your servant? I'd heard that he was responsible, yet the report we currently have dismissed that theory." The suspicion was gone now, replaced by curiosity.

"Yes, it had been fabricated. Currently, he is missing. I had been injured and I'm afraid I don't know what happened before I woke."

"I am glad to see you have recovered then. It is a shame. Your family's reign has always been known for its servants, among your other accomplishments."

"Thank you, Sir."

He watched the king escort his daughter away. Interesting. He'd approved of the union for the benefits to the kingdom, but it looked like Eudora would be a decent match for the prince. After a few years, of course.

By the time he excused himself from the festivities and obligatory introductions, dancing, drinks, and feasting, he was exhausted. He spotted Maddox, waiting patiently by the doors and he nodded his head to the priest.

"Pastor." He glanced around, assured that no one was listening. "Thank you."

Maddox eyed him up and down, a strange expression painted over his face. "You have nothing to thank me for, Your Majesty. I did nothing. Absolutely nothing."

Evander tilted his head to the side, slowly putting meaning to those words. "But…"

"It would seem that Vladimir was not so celibate after all." The priest bowed and left before he could respond.

It made too much sense for Evander to even attempt to dissuade himself. Why his direct bloodline were somehow always the ones chosen as the Guardians, why Ansom would have risked so much. If he could have proved that he was a legitimate heir, then it would have made securing the throne almost easy.

# Chapter Fifteen
Month of the Crab 29, 423 HE

Evander sat at his desk, the large study too quiet as he shifted through trade agreements and local reports.

It had been two years. The first had flown by in a blur between his recovery, his coronation, and enforcing the new laws protecting magic users. He'd had to increase the number of soldiers assigned to each of the provinces. The abolishing of the anti-magic law had sparked a witch-hunt.

Many ability users who revealed themselves were killed; others began openly wreaking havoc with their magic. The soldiers were ordered to uphold the laws of the kingdom and Evander was pleased that they seemed to be holding true to that ideal. Those who openly murdered the ability users were apprehended on charges of murder. Those ability users who were causing harm with their magic were brought up on appropriate charges as well.

It was stressful and chaotic, but he stuck to his view, adapting his approach as necessary, and it had paid off. The tension had calmed after a year and a half of constant enforcement. He sighed and rubbed a hand over his face. He was… tired. His gaze slid to the ornate music box that sat on the corner of the desk.

*"Your Majesty, what did you expect to find here?" Sir Hayden asked as they trudged up the path towards the Shors Pass Manor.*

*"I'm not entirely sure," he replied. "By the way, did you remember to bring the sweets I asked for?"*

*"Yes, Your Majesty," Sir Hayden sighed.*

*"Could you check, please? I'd rather not get there only to realize we forgot them."*

*He waited until the soldier stopped and turned to take off the pack he was carrying. While his back was turned, Evander stepped into a nearby shadow, sinking into it and popping up around the corner, out of sight of the man.*

*Thankfully, his ability hadn't left him when he switched bodies, however it did get weaker. He couldn't control shadows as he used to. Able to move through them, but unable to pull them and move them to his will. He shook his head as he heard Hayden's exclamation and stepped into another shadow. He made it to the door of the manor a full ten minutes before the soldier.*

*He didn't bother knocking, turning the handle and pushing against the door, surprised when it slid open.*

*Only to reveal an abandoned house.*

*He stepped inside, listening to the silence as his footsteps sent up small puffs of dust. He'd hoped that Malik would still be here, that Riu had brought Caiden here. He watched the motes of dust swirl through the beams of light that pierced the gloom of the building. He set his foot on the stairs and made his way up to the Music Room.*

*All of those memories, gone. He stared at the empty shelves, then he spotted it: his inheritance. The music box sat on the desk. He picked it up, gingerly lifting the lid only to find it empty. The key wasn't there. He stared at it for a moment. He couldn't deny the hurt that filled him. He understood it, after all. He'd gone through so many of Malik's memories that he'd gotten a feel for the man's way of thinking.*

*He had failed. He'd survived, but he failed to protect his charge. Caiden had fallen. Perhaps the Prince had died after all. Either way, he would never know what memory had been gifted to him.*

*"You-Your Majesty... what the hell...?" Sir Hayden panted as he stumbled into the room. He must have run the entire way after losing him.*

*"Apologies, Sir Hayden. It would seem it was a fruitless venture. Let us go home." Evander closed the box and brushed past him.*

*He could feel the man watching him as he descended the stairs.*

*"Your Majesty..."*

*He turned to look up at the knight.*

*"I don't know what you expected to find here."*
*He gestured loosely around the clearly abandoned*
*house. "But I am sorry."*

*Had he really been so obvious? He stared at his*
*footprints that had been left in the dust. He couldn't tell*
*if he was disappointed because of the memory, or*
*because he had been hoping to find Caiden.*

*"It was a pointless hope to begin with." He*
*chuckled, stifling the persistent lump that burned in his*
*throat. "But thank you."*

He ran his fingers over the smooth wood, a sense
of heart-wrenching yearning filling him for a moment
before a knock broke him out of his thoughts.

"Enter."

The door opened to reveal Sir Hayden, his battle
master in full now, since the previous battle master had
been killed during the coup. He'd become somewhat of a
confidant, staying near him and acting as a bodyguard
since the Vladimir clan was still rebuilding.

Honestly, Evander was lucky to have the soldier
at his side. Sir Hayden's group was one of the very few
to survive the coup. Ansom had used the castle's
defenses to slaughter those who would later cause him
trouble, leaving only those loyal to him or those whom
he could manipulate. Without Sir Hayden's help,
Evander was sure he would have lost the figurative battle
with the council and nobility that had remained after
Ansom was declared a traitor. Not to say they were all
against him, many hadn't been at the castle during the

coup and were therefore safe but also were only aware of what Ansom had told them. Many had been convinced that Ansom was the good guy through all of this.

*Ah, there's a thought.* Perhaps he'd rework the defenses, make a failsafe on the inside so anyone escaping the castle could get out and not be trapped. There were still bloodstains in the killing yard, the first before the castle itself. No one had even made it past that first — what was supposed to be the last — line of defense. It made his stomach turn thinking of how many people Ansom would have had to have on his side to accomplish such massacre.

Evander shook his head, still amazed by it years later. *No.* He reminded himself that one would only need a small handful of people to man the murder holes and traps. Even just one combative ability user could kill such a tightly packed panicking mob. That was the point of the yards after all.

*Damn.* A failsafe on the inside would render the whole thing useless. He'd just have to hope something like that never happened again. At least not under his watch.

This was something that crossed his mind on a regular basis and he easily pushed it away as Sir Hayden closed the door behind him and saluted.

"You may sit, Sir Hayden. What brings you to me?"

"Your Majesty, if I may. It has been two years. You need to marry."

*Well, that was certainly to the point.* Evander sighed and leaned back in his chair. "As I've said before,

Sir Hayden, I simply do not feel comfortable marrying until things within the kingdom become stable again." He'd had several meetings with Eudora, just pleasantries. She was slowly starting to drop her guard, letting more of her personality show through.

He had expressed interest in her, keeping the promise of their engagement alive, but continued to avoid the topic of marriage. After all, it wasn't his place to make that decision for Caiden, not to mention a wedding was something that one should experience for themselves.

"Things are as stable as they are going to get, Your Majesty. I am speaking for the Council as well when I express my concern for your status."

"I have already made my opinion clear on the matter. I will not marry until the kingdom is stable."

There was silence again.

"Until the kingdom is stable? Or until Caiden comes back?"

Evander's gaze immediately went to the soldier. "Excuse me?" As much as he liked him, Evander was certainly not opposed to killing the man.

"Caiden would never rest until Evander was found. I know that for a fact. I don't know what happened, I don't know why, but I know you aren't Caiden. Evander, on the other hand? I thought it was strange from the moment you woke up how similar you were to him. So, I'll ask again. What are you waiting for?"

Evander stared at him, but it quickly became apparent that Hayden wasn't going to drop it. "I can't make a decision like that for him. I won't. I'm just trying to keep things together until he comes back."

"And if he doesn't come back? I'm not trying to force you into anything, but the Council is still trying to take back the control that they've lost. If they see this as an opportunity..."

Evander was about to reply when a servant burst into the room.

"Uh, beg your pardon, Your Majesty, but there is a group of magic users in the throne room. They want to speak with you. They were quite forceful."

Evander rose to his feet, sharing a look with Sir Hayden, wondering if it was Riu or Karen or perhaps it was some of the Vladimir clan who'd escaped now trying to return. There had been several cases of that already.

Evander smothered the hope that rose in his chest. It was likely a small group of the Vladimir clan returning to their positions. Still, he couldn't help it. He made his way to the throne room at a quick pace. He paused outside the doors, straightening his clothes and waiting for Hayden to catch up.

The soldier opened the doors and stood aside while the herald announced his presence to the gathered people. Evander kept his eyes forward, refusing to look and let that small hope be crushed so soon. He settled into the throne, relaxed in the overly large chair, reclining as he looked over the assembled magic users. His eyes widened at the sight of Riu's smirking face.

Five people were gathered in front of him. Karen, Riu and three others that must have joined them. Yet, no Caiden. He supposed he would have been notified if 'Evander' returned. He was still wanted alive.

He swallowed, struggling to maintain a calm demeanor. "Guards. You are all dismissed."

There was muttering as they stood there, confused. "Uh, Your Majesty?"

"Leave. Sir Hayden will stay with me. I have something I wish to discuss with these people."

"As you wish, Sire." The reply was slow and clearly, they were unwilling to leave him in the presence of so many ability users who may or may not be hostile, but Evander couldn't think of a better way to get rid of them.

The doors closed, and he stood about to demand where Caiden was.

"The rumors were true; I do look good on that throne." The light, off-handed comment drew his attention to a shadowed corner of the room. At first, he didn't see the speaker until the darkness abruptly dispersed, the shadows seeming to flee the man as he stepped forward.

The entire room seemed to get brighter, the shade being pushed rather than pulled, and Evander belatedly realized that his ability was being used to move the shadow's *away*. It barely processed as he watched a grin spread across his own face.

"What? No witty reply? C'mon, Eva, I'm a bit disappointed." Caiden grinned.

"Told you I'd bring him back." Riu's voice smugly inserted itself while he stood in shock. He couldn't form the words and finally Caiden's expression softened. He couldn't bring himself to speak.

Caiden strode up to him, looking up at him with a slight smile, "Eva, you look like you're going to cry. Are you that upset to see me?"

"I hate you so much." Finally, his voice broke through as he gave in and hugged the man.

# Epilogue

"Your Majesty, the King of Terravinter will be arriving shortly. Preparations have concluded."

"Mhmm."

"Your daughter is requesting that you meet with her before he arrives to approve of her dress."

"Mhmm."

"Your kingdom is burning."

"Mhmm."

Evander finally stopped and glared at the king sitting at his desk, idly playing with the shadow cast by the inkwell. His hair held a few streaks of grey now, premature after a few years of dealing with pirate raids. He couldn't help sighing as he waited for Caiden to realize that he'd stopped talking.

Forty years of age and still acting like a child.

"Hey, Eva."

"Yes, Your Majesty?"

"There's still an hour or so before my father-in-law arrives, correct?"

"Yes...?" He didn't hide the suspicion in his voice.

"Could you tell the guards to notify me when he gets here?"

Evander frowned. "Of course, Your Majesty." He slowly walked to the door, poking his head outside to relay the King's orders. He thought that maybe the room got darker for a moment and sighed as he turned back to Caiden.

Only to find the king gone.

He couldn't stop the grin that stole across his features, a chuckle echoing in the now-empty study. Some things never changed.

*The blood of the covenant is thicker than the water of the womb.*

# Vladimir Family Tree

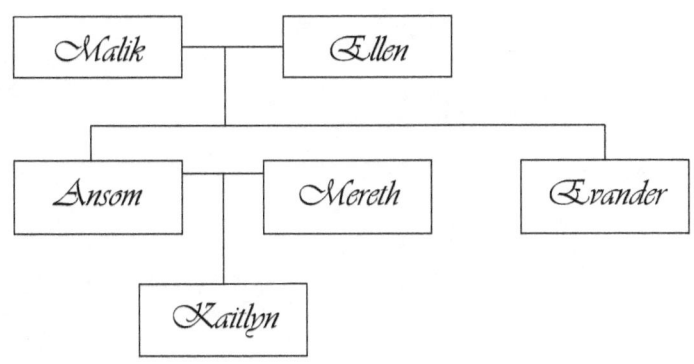

# Kailyn Family Tree

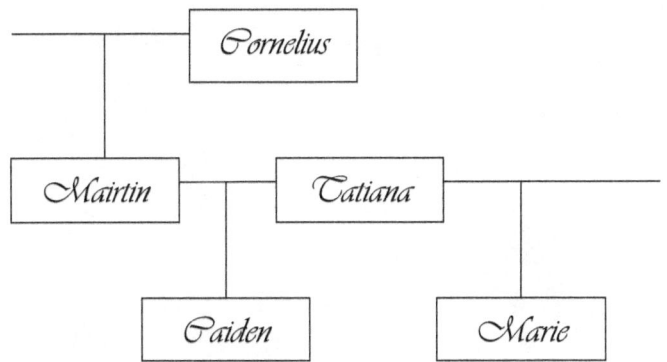

# Acknowledgments

Well, it took long enough, but here we are. Thank you to all my poor, hapless friends and family who were pestered endlessly into reading. And re-reading. Over and over again.

A million and one thank yous to Ashley Elliott, for the guidance and trail blazing in the realm of self-publishing. To Leia, for dealing with me and my ranting all the time. Also, to Alison, who was unafraid to rip the entire work apart and help me put it back together again (much better this time around). To Paul for doctoring it up and helping get everything into shape.

To all my lovely victims – I mean test readers, I couldn't have done it without you guys.

# About the Author

Macie Cage is a book hoarder with an unsustainable caffeine addiction. Her hobbies include crocheting, video games, and obsessively playing pen and paper RPGs. Hobbies definitely do <u>not</u> include attempting to talk about herself in the third person. She resides in the suburbs of Pittsburgh with too many ideas and not nearly enough time.

SHADOW DANCER is her first work to survive long enough to be published.

<u>VISIT & FOLLOW</u>
www.maciecage.com
Twitter: @MacieCage
Facebook: Macie Cage

www.ingramcontent.com/pod-product-compliance
Lightning Source LLC
Chambersburg PA
CBHW022134240626
47153CB00007B/2363